Relief with a Sob

ALBAN NWAKIRE AZUWIKE

PARTRIDGE
A Penguin Random House Company

To order additional copies of this book, contact
Toll Free 0800 990 914 (South Africa)
+44 20 3014 3997 (outside South Africa)
orders.africa@partridgepublishing.com

www.partridgepublishing.com/africa

DEDICATION

To my dear wife, Theresa who generously and unconditionally granted me leave of absence from her regular companionship for several years which enabled me to put in the form of novel my eccentric ideas and imaginations.

CHAPTER 1

The director of education returned from the governor's office weather-beaten and confused after a five-hour meeting with the governor, the commissioner for education and the permanent secretary in the Ministry of Education. There was a lot of pressure to make him agree to the prevalent belief in the ministry high quarters that education budget was too high and needed to be trimmed down to square with the deteriorating finances of the state government. He pressed the inter-com bell on his table and a frail girl emerged from an adjoining room normally manned by a receptionist and a messenger.

"Edina", he called, trying to brighten up, "call me my secretary." Tell him to bring his note book along."

She opened a door at right angles with the one from which she emerged. In a matter of seconds, the secretary surfaced.

"Sir", answered the secretary, extremely anxious to please. "Sit down, Jim and take a dictation. The heading is: "A Memo to the Honorable Commissioner for Education."

"With reference to our discussion this afternoon, I am afraid I must insist that we do not cut down allocation to education. I sincerely believe, and I hope you share my views, that for our projected development plan to have a semblance of reality, we have to have a strong and reliable educational system. I also believe that unless we ensure a strong foundation, we are building on sand. I yet do not understand how we can convince ourselves and the general public that our primary schools remain grossly ill-equipped and under-staffed, thirty years after the Nigerian Civil War. Secondary schools are not better either. Even the newly-built community schools, most of them located in remote villages, do not have adequate staffing."

"Please use your good office to persuade the governor to rethink on the issue."

The memo was securely placed on the commissioner's table an hour later. Pensively studying the content of a file, the commissioner took no notice of the person who delivered the memo. He was about to leave office for that day when his eyes stumbled on the bold print "VERY

URGENT" stamped on the top right edge of the envelope bearing the dissent. He picked it up, pulled out the content and scanned it quickly, heaved a big sigh, then sat down and read it again more slowly. His near-bursting bile duct diffused itself, and he relaxed on his chair, dropping the memo carelessly. His reverie was disturbed by his messenger who felt it was time to ensure that the office security system was in order before everybody vacated it.

"Never mind, Chidi; you can go."

The duty-weary man was very grateful. "Thank you sir," he replied as he dashed out.

The honourable gentleman was in a dilemma. Being an educationist, he knew the weaknesses of the edifice he was lured in to prop up. He had had a frank discussion on it with the governor before the top-level meeting. During the private discussion, he earnestly and expertly tried to impress on the governor the need to radically restructure the existing educational machinery. The governor's brusque reply was stunning. He had only two options: accept the sacrosanct and 'realistic' assessment of the situation by veteran ministry officials or hand in his resignation. He treasured his job more than he valued refined views. As a face-saving solution, he answered: "His Excellency, I will give it a serious thought, bear with me".

This God-damned memo had thrust back on him the sickening dilemma. Should he now throw in the towel and finish with the well organised but self-condemning pretence, or should he continue to stage-manage the drama in spite of the dwindling ovation?

Before he left his office late that evening, he resolved the matter. In a situation like mine, there is little room for finesse. This is a lucrative job I did not campaign for. At the expiration of my tenure, I will not hope to have the opportunity again. Why not cow-tow for the remaining period and leave the re-organisation for a future commissioner when the time will perhaps be auspicious? He then quietly drafted a reply memo before leaving his office. The following morning, the reply was typed, signed and delivered to the director promptly.

It was crisp and sharp. "Referring to your memo of yesterday, putting the precarious financial situation around us and the political nature of our job into consideration, I frankly advise that you abide by our collective decision or seek direct audience with the governor. In the alternative, tender your resignation or better still, apply for re-assignment since you are part of the system, unlike me."

Going through the commissioner's letter, the director's drooping spirit found expression in a soliloquy: "Well I did what I had done to liberate my conscience. I never for one moment, hoped I would influence change or modification of the policy. Let us continue flattering ourselves."

Thank you for purchasing a copy of
Relief With a Sob.
By purchasing this book you contribute
to the Azuwike family mission to bring
free secondary education to children
in Nkalu village in South-eastern
Nigeria.

For further enquiries or
to purchase more copies,
please email
frokechukwu@yahoo.com

or call:

1(731)4385877 - USA
+1(647)9285855 - Canada
+(234)8063621191 - Nigeria

He looked up, his face beclouded with gloom, and discovered that he was talking to himself, and that the last person he would communicate his views on the matter to, his messenger, was standing by, awaiting orders.

"Philip, did I send for you?" he asked, startled.

"No sir, I am here just in case. I placed the letter from the commissioner on your table."

"You can leave for the mean time. I have no engagement for you right now."

He wanted to attend to other matters but concentration deserted him. He skimmed through three files but none made any sense to him. Some steam must be let off in order to allow concentration to sit in. Getting up from his seat, he pressed the bell and Philip popped in.

"I am going to the bank in case there is a phone call from the governor or commissioner. I will be back around 12.00 noon. Get my driver at once".

The driver was fetched and they drove away. In less than thirty minutes, he was through with the bank, then ordered the driver to take him to "Coco-nut Inn." There he ordered fried gizzard and a bottle of coke. As he munched his choice meat and washed it down with chilled coke, sobriety returned to him. He realized that his own view of prosperity was incompatible with the inordinate quest for wealth that was so characteristic of the society in which he lived and worked. If he was kicked out of office as a result of his disinterested single-handed move to improve the educational system, he wouldn't have the sympathy of the public. The commissioner was right. It would cost him nothing to uphold the collective decision. After all, how many of his children were or would ever be, in the public school system?

An expanded top-level meeting was re-convened in the Ministry of Education three weeks later. This time it was addressed by the commissioner for education and attended, in addition to the three chief executive directors in the different departments of education, chief inspectors of education and outsiders whose professional advice would be invaluable, like head of the Department of Education in the same college.

At the end of the grandiloquent marathon address, the attendants were more confused than convinced of the appropriateness of the projected extensive innovation in the educational system. Statistics were extensively employed which dampened the listeners' interest rather than clarify matters. The address left little room for questioning, and indeed, a few questions were allowed to complete formality. The dignitaries invited from outside found it more proper to concur than advice. Some of the attendants concentrated more on the sweet-sounding language of the commissioner than on the whole reason for the meeting. Every attendant, with very few exceptions, was satisfied with one aspect of the address or another.

Faithful to his duty as the chief policy maker and propagandist for the Ministry of Information, the relevant excerpts from his address under the caption: "State Education System Refurbished". The following morning, it made the front page headline in the state-owned newspaper. Not only giving it adequate coverage, it was also the editorial topic. The editor eulogized, not only the forward-looking personality of the state governor and his lieutenants in the various ministries but also the dynamic nature of the education policy and planners in the state, concluding it with, "At last the tax-payers' aspiration for qualitative education for their children has been realized."

The press coverage inadvertently proved to be ambivalent. Glamorous as the new plan appeared, certain pit-falls of it failed to escape public scrutiny. People wondered what would become of the Teacher Training Colleges (TTC) that would no longer be peopled from the beginning of the next academic year, and the products of the functioning ones since an embargo on the employment of new grade II teachers was embodied in the innovation, while the more critical minds wondered about the rationale of an educational improvement program which encouraged perpetual scarcity of staff at the root of education. The editorial of an independent weekly paper, renowned for its forthrightness in matters people were wary to make comments on, called it a coup de -grace to the ramshackle edifice.

There was, however, a plausible aspect – the retraining of serving grade II teachers, christened "T.C. I course". Referring to it, the state-owned paper extolled the "discerning qualities of our very hard-working and unrivaled commissioner for education whose quick action was found to stem the tide of depreciating educational standards". In the eyes of the field officers of education namely, teachers' trainers in the depreciating institutions, the retraining program deserved commendation in view of the fact that most of the experienced trained teachers had slipped into progressive regression to illiteracy for abandoning reading, while the new products left college certificated but unskilled enough for effective teaching. The so-called crash program for training teachers introduced much earlier, bears a large portion of the blame for the professional and academic quackery.

The curriculum development section of the Ministry of Education had been given the task of producing in record time, a syllabus for the different subjects to be offered in the T.C. I course, officers on leave in the department were recalled and overtime allowances guaranteed for every cadre of teachers.

Meanwhile the chief inspector of education in the teacher training section, an eloquent young man, had been dispatched to shuttle between the selected colleges for the course and address staff and students on the new roles of the colleges, the need for the course, the requirements and preparations before take-off. In one of such briefing sessions, one teacher asked him to explain the sense in retaining one or two colleges to continue churning out T.C. II teachers who wouldn't be employed.

"That is an irrelevant question", he grunted. "I have just talked on the new T.C. I course. What has continuing T.C. II got to do with it?"

"Let me answer it sir," threw in another teacher.

"Perhaps to produce teachers to be retrained later."

"A very ingenuous answer", contributed the principal of the college. "But we have just heard that the course is for serving teachers."

In an attempt to forestall more of such embarrassing questions, the chief concluded: "If you feel strongly about continuing T.C. II course or the fate of your products, the door of the director of education is always open to enquirers."

In another encounter elsewhere, in spite of his captivating oratory and evasive techniques, the embarrassing question re-surfaced in a slightly different form: "Sir, the T.C. I course is laudable. The middle manpower required to cope with the secondary school phase of our 6:3:3:4 program will thus be mass-produced and cheaply though."

"Not so cheaply," corrected the chief. "The teachers in training will be paid their salaries. That perhaps explains why non-serving teachers are not eligible. There will be no basis for paying them salaries."

"To continue my question sir, the refined personnel will be deployed in junior secondary schools, thereby depleting the already weak staff of primary schools, yet there will be no new recruitment to fill the vacuum that will be created. Isn't the government robbing Peter to pay Paul, or rather emptying one bottle to fill another?"

"I don't know who is robbing whom or emptying a bottle. The education of our children is the main concern of our government. How can government undercut that? I think it is a matter of placing emphasis where the need is stark. In any case, you can always have a chat with the director of education or the honorable commissioner. Both are very approachable gentlemen."

One of the female officers who accompanied him had permission to stress one of the requirements. She approached it in a rather humorous way.

"My dear students, I can see that the teaching profession, perhaps at the primary school level, seems to have been taken over by the female gender. That isn't bad;

women nurse children in their homes, so they carry the patronizing attitude over to the school. Nevertheless my fellow women I have to make a special appeal to your will-power. If anyone is found with a baby during the course, she will be made to withdraw at once."

A female student summoned nerves to ask: "Even if she is married?"

"Yes, married women will have to agree with their husbands before enrolling and we shall require them to produce letters of consent from their husbands. If any couple's priority is rearing children, the female partner had better not apply."

A teacher on the staff of the college struck what he thought was a compromise. "What you are stressing madam, may not apply in our college. The two courses that will be taught here are so strenuous that such incidents will be rare here."

"I wouldn't subscribe to that idea", replied the officer. "I am not a medical officer but let me warn that you do not under-rate women in matters affecting mother craft". Roars of laughter.

As the visitors drove away, one female student remarked to a group of fellow female students; "It is women who will witch-hunt fellow women. Most of them in the ministries have had their fill in marriage pleasures and child bearing. A few are divorced or not married at all. It is they who preach utter restraint in marital relationships."

Everyone in the group shared her views but agreed that there was always a way out. One of them remarked: "If one conceives three months or less before the end of her course, how would they discover it unless they subject us to medical tests which they will not dare."

Another one cut in, "What has a vulture got to do with a barber? The government has already declared us contraband even before we fail the impending T.C. II examination. Let us forget the gold-mine of a course and work for the examination we are going to do in two months time. One only hopes it will survive T.C. II too long. The financial constraint which doomed T.C. II will eventually catch up with T.C. I."

Another one added: "Didn't they make the same laws about our own course? So far only very few careless women have fallen victim to the law. I know a woman who hid pregnancy here for six months. She had her baby barely four weeks after her last paper."

"Some of us, added yet another, have difficulty in getting pregnant. If God answers our prayers during the course, do we terminate the pregnancy in obedience to a facile law or do they mean that throughout the course, married couples should abstain from sex? Whichever they mean is their business. Every woman should know how to go about her marriage responsibilities."

The consensus was that male principals were more understanding than their female counterparts. It was, therefore, advisable to confide in the former if one found oneself in such a problem. Chances were that they might cover up any such situation tacitly. Women take interest in exposing fellow women.

CHAPTER II

Miss Lucy Iweh had stayed idle for more than two years since being trained as a teacher. All the time she had been at home, doing a lot of odd services in her family. Just to relieve boredom, she sought her father's permission to spend a month or two with her elder brother, a trader at Aba. On boarding a vehicle, she ran into a former course mate of hers.

"Hello Chinwe", she greeted. "How is life?"

"It couldn't be worse", replied Chinwe. "In the last year of our course, I was anxious to leave college. Now I wish I could start all over again. I am fed up with everything at home. I am not bright enough to pass the University entrance examination. Even if one passes it, are parents prepared to continue investing on one person when other children are coming up? So I continue wasting precious time at home with very little hope of ever getting relief from any quarters."

"My sister, your lot is not a singular one. All of us products of Teacher Training Colleges (TTC's) have the same plight."

"I don't believe all of us have equal plight. Some lucky girls have been comfortably married. Some others have been employed in private nursery schools and are sure of their toiletries at least."

"Do not grieve because you haven't been employed in a private school. You are better off not employed in any of them. A couple of weeks ago, I saw Rose Ugwu at a wedding ceremony; you remember her, the best girl at mathematics in our class."

"Yes, I do. Where is she now? I thought she had got entry into the University long ago. How I wish I had her brains."

Which University? She is languishing in one of your pet nursery schools. She is paid only eight hundred naira a month for mothering over one hundred and fifty babies, I mean babies. Often against her will, she is taken out by her boss. Her parents are not well-to-do enough to sponsor her university education, and her employer promises to do that, hence she licks his boots. You know she loves higher education."

"Poor girl! How I wish she had rich parents. The so-called employers these days have become very callous and unreliable. We girls are unfortunate. At every turn we are susceptible to unfair exploitation. When will our state government lift the ban on employment of grade II teachers?"

"When we have reverted to illiteracy or been rendered unmarriageable as a result of hardship which can lead one astray? Whichever girl you see in this state, it is the same story of disguised unemployment and exploitation. Indeed we are taken three for a kobo. Who takes the blame – ourselves, the employers or our government?"

The relief package was announced with fanfare by all the news media in the state. More pleasant still, the employment was going to be localized. Every intending employee was to apply to their local government for employment, primary schools having been given over to local government council for management. The editorial column of the state-owned paper made a passionate appeal to the education units of the local government areas to carry out the exercise with compassion and dispatch, concluding the appeal with: "In a situation where a teacher controlling two hundred pupils is the rule rather than the exception, the need to employ more teachers without delay can hardly be over emphasised."

Back home at the various local government headquarters, walls and tree trunks were emblazoned with posters with the following inscription: "Vacancies exist in the primary schools system for certificated grade II teachers. Intending candidates should apply, stating, among other things, their local government area of origin, and year of certification, and enclosing an identification letter from their traditional ruler and twenty naira application fee in postal or money order. Applications should reach the Head, Education Unit, not later than one month from the date of this publication."

In their wards councilors amplified the advertisement. Curious applicants, wishing to have an edge over others, approached the councilors for guidance, often edged on by their parents and relations. One Luke Ijere had a very good result – almost credits all through. Naturally he rated his chances very high and so did not bother about seeing any councilor. One morning, his father called:

"Luke, you don't seem to be interested in the Advertised employment prospect. Perhaps you have got a job or are about securing one."

"How do you mean father? Are you saying this because I did not ask you for the application fee? I felt for you and decided to save you the trouble."

"Yes, not only not asking for the application fee, you don't make any move. Applicants are running shifts at councilor Ike's house. I remember you were very enthusiastic in campaigning for him when he was contesting election. However, thank you for saving me the twenty naira expense."

"Yes I was very enthusiastic indeed and that is a more reason why he should lobby for me whether I consult him or not. What I thought I needed to do was to let him know that I applied, and that I did the very day I handed in my application. Isn't that enough?"

"Not quite, Luke. You have to be in touch with him from time to time so that you will be abreast of the latest developments. This is our country. The current of events moves so fast that toddlers are easily swept off their feet. I have to warn here that you should not place much hope on the election services you rendered to Mr. Ike. Once election fever is over, both successful and unsuccessful candidates forget those who suffered for them. You are too young yet to have experienced it."

"I think you are right, father, but my result is so good that interviewers cannot so unfeelingly discountenance it unless our society has degenerated to that abyss of corruption. However, I will contact him very soon."

A few days later, Luke was squatting uneasily on a chair in his father's living room, telling a different story.

"Father, you have a wonderful insight into the happenings on our country. Our society is a frustrating one. I doubt whether I have any chances."

"What happened?" asked his father anxiously.

"I spent more than two hours with councilor Ike today. As soon as he saw me, he railed at me for keeping complacently away." I am quoting his words. He asked: "Do you pride yourself on your result? There are better ones. In any case, good or excellent result, every successful grade II trained teacher is eligible, and it doesn't follow that a good result makes one a good teacher. That is how the council reasons about it. Let me reveal this to you, the council will treat every candidate on equal footing, irrespective of quality of certificate."

"Sir, I complied with the requirements of the advertisement. Besides, I thought I should spare you headaches if I avoided importunity with you."

"That was very good of you but this is not an affair between one person and another. Councilors will handle the recruitment exercise collectively, and they have set down their conditions. Perhaps I might make yet another revelation to you. We have much fewer chances than the number of application so far received. It follows that not all applicants will be employed. Some of my fellow Councilors are hell-bent on recruiting on the basis of the highest bidder despite pressure from a few of us who see the applicants as pitiable."

"What is one supposed to do then?" Asked Luke, growing despondent.

"Every applicant has to offer some "kola" (bribe) but that is not the end of it. Your councilor sponsor has to lobby hard for you, and that entails more spending. Councilors have to give drinks occasionally in order to get them listen to your appeal."

"Could you, sir, give me an idea of the value of the 'kola'?"

It isn't terribly much but quite staggering for poor village folk. It is only a thousand five hundred naira, including the lobbying expenses."

"How soon is one supposed to offer the "kola" and to whom?"

"There is no deadline but it must be at least a week before the interview. The councilor from your ward is the right person to channel it through."

"Good night sir, Let me go and consult my father. You will be hearing from me very soon."

"Good bye. I will do my best for you."

His father was less surprised than worried about how to raise the money. "That is our reward for voting in the so-called right candidates. I am not convinced that the council will demand as much as one thousand five hundred naira. You can be sure that the extra five hundred naira is for Mr. Ike. We are refunding the few naira he gave to each of us who voted him, our campaign efforts completely forgotten."

"Father, you are perfectly right for he said he was going to spend money lobbying other councilors. What an ungrateful man!"

Councilor Orji summoned a meeting of town Union Chairman and village heads in his ward, at his residence a week after the media had given wide publicity to the rare job opportunities offered to prospective teachers. At five 0'clock p.m. on the appointed day, his sitting room was brim-full with attendants. All the available seats having been taken up, late comers perched on the padded arms of settees. The two bottles of whisky he presented had been licked to the last drop before half the number turned up. The two empty bottles were left standing on the round centre table to speak for themselves instead of the host apologizing for kola, and none of the late-comers dared ask for kola since they had themselves to blame for missing the very costly one presented.

The councilor stood up to address his guests. "Thanks a lot for responding promptly to my summons. It is a sure sign that our political awareness campaign has taken roots. Having kindly elected me your representative in our local government council, you have made me your ear in government quarters. I would be doing you a grave disservice or failing in my obligation to you if I withheld any bit of useful information from you. Most probably you have all heard of the advertised vacancies for unemployed trained teachers. I wanted to ensure this and make some necessary explanations. Government has come to our door-steps. That is why some of us believe in spite of the general feeling, that the present civilian regime is indeed the people's government. Not only increasing the number of local government areas, thus spreading development to rural areas (our local government headquarters being a living example), local governments are given more powers and more funds with a view to quickening the tempo of rural development. They are also made independent of state governments and receive direct grants from the Federal Government so as to avoid the erstwhile diversion of funds by state governments to suit their priorities which invariably retarded the efforts of local government."

"As you must have known, primary schools are now to be controlled by local governments, a sort of division of labour, you know: the federal government controlling tertiary institutions while the state governments take charge of secondary schools and teacher-training colleges."

The rehearsal type of fluency impressed most of his listeners.

"We shall equip schools, employ and pay the staff, control the transfer of teachers and discipline bad ones. When the state government staffed primary schools, a teacher could be sent to a place more than thirty kilometers from his home. He had little option since he did not know whom to protest to. Even if he went to the State Education Board headquarters, identifying the right officer would take him a whole working day. Even then there was little guarantee that his case would have any more attention as soon as he left the officer's room. If he attempted bribing, the money more often than not, got into the wrong hands making his efforts futile. Now that the whole operation is brought home to us, one can easily go to a place of one's choice."

With a broad smile depicting a readiness to serve and a feeling of self-importance, he added: "Make use of your councilor. It is my duty to minister to your needs as far as the local government is concerned."

Having enjoyed the unvoiced gratitude radiated on the faces of many of the guests, he lowered his voice as though he wanted to take them into confidence: "You know nowadays nothing goes for nothing. Some of my fellow councilors are retired teachers. When we started teaching, our monthly salary was less than twenty naira. Grade II teachers, regarded as the highest grade of primary school teachers, were paid about hundred naira. Today a grade II teacher starts on a salary of more than a thousand naira per month which is much higher than my total emolument as a teacher. The days of poor teachers are gone for ever. Teachers draw allowances like civil servants and enjoy other fringe benefits. In view of all these and the pain of working round the clock on their behalf, the council has decided that every applicant must pay an application fee of one thousand naira through his councilor and this must reach the council before the interview day."

As he said this, he looked round cautiously, hoping to read their reaction on their faces.

"Excuse me councilor", requested one of the guests. "I read the advertisement in the "Daily Post" and heard it over the radio. It was neither explicitly stated nor implicitly mooted that applicants should pay any application fee. Would you, therefore, guarantee that we shall be given receipts if we make the payment?"

Everybody turned to the direction of the questioner. Definitely everybody got the councilors message perfectly right. The introductory sentence dispelled ambiguity, so 'Mr. Wiseman' looked foolish in the eyes of a majority of the assembled men. However, a few elderly men who still attached some importance to morality gave him unexpressed support.

Councilor Orji had some difficulty making up his mind what to say in reply. Not that he regarded bribery as immoral or unlawful or that he felt caught in a tight corner. The problem was that Mr. Iwuji who asked the question was his senior in the teaching profession and rendered him immense help both by way of giving him lessons and offering him advice in the face of difficulty. Besides, his reputation as an honest and hard working teacher lingered on years after his retirement. If the challenge had come from the commoners, he would have used the opportunity to teach the guests speech etiquette. In any case, he would not allow prolonged silence to give way to opprobrious sneering. As if recovering his poise suddenly, he made an acrobatic swing of his head in the direction of the question.

"No Mr. Iwuji. The application fee is not spelt out in the media but I can assure you every local government council in our state orally inserted that clause. You can make enquiries in the neighbouring local government areas. In fact in some local government areas. the fee is much higher than that. You will surely expect no official receipt from the council, but if you insist on getting one, when you make the payment to me, I will personally give it to you."

One impatient listener in the group discarded decorum.

"Councilor," he interposed, "ignore him. I know he has no son or daughter wanting employment. He wants to spoil the chances of poor people's children. The councilor has given us the message he was mandated to spread to his people. He didn't fabricate it. If anyone feels strongly about it, let him go to the council secretary or chairman for authentication."

Mr. Iwuji chose to remain indifferent and silent, contrary to the general expectation of the crowd. Councilor Orji struck a compromise chord: "Mr. Iwuji has a right to be correctly informed. I do not believe that asking well-intentioned questions will jeopardize one's children's chances of recruitment. However, a councilor who didn't know Mr. Iwuji's background would have frowned at the question."

A few more questions, all of them invariably trivial, were asked before the meeting came to a close. As the guests walked home, a heated argument erupted between self appointed agents of councilors and those who felt aggrieved by the unwanted exhortation from poor village folk. Most vocal among the councilor's defenders was ironically a literate young man who naturally was expected to condemn bribery and corruption unequivocally. He was a serving officer in the civil service. He shouted with quasi mock exasperation: "I dislike your hypocritical disposition. Is the fee unlawful because councilors are asking for it? How many of you questioned the lawfulness or otherwise of the fees you demanded from them before casting your votes for them? Can you imagine how much each spent in order to be your councilors?"

There followed an angry rejoinder: "Who asked for their money? They desperately needed the votes in the face of stiff competition amongst them, the contestants, and gave out the money without being asked to do so."

"Why didn't you reject it and vote according to your conscience? Now you want their votes in a different situation, and you have to buy them very exorbitantly. What do you think is their sitting allowance, and how many years will they stay in office before they recover lawfully all they spent? Just in the same way as one good turn deserves another, one bad turn begets another. Stop complaining. When you allow your conscience to guide your actions, we shall enjoy a clean society. Till then let us brace ourselves to bear the consequences of our avarice."

Another defender of the council introduced a new dimension. "We have tactlessly legalized giving and receiving of 'tips' popularly known as kola. Everyone of us has mortgaged his conscience to the pursuit of material wealth. The other day, I went to a magistrate court to swear to affidavits for people applying for travel passports. The oaths clerk went through the forms I handed to him, nodded in approval and told me that the fee was two naira per form. I gave him a five naira note which he pocketed without making any attempt to give a change. After stamping and endorsing the forms, he looked at my face and said, "It remains wine fee". Not being in the mood for argument, I asked him how much the wine fee was.

"Any amount you choose to offer, sir."

I gave him another five naira. Then he wrote out official receipts for the forms and gave the receipts and the forms to me. I denied him the official courtesy of "thank you very much." Was it the council that demanded or authorized that? Now every facet of our life is stinking with corruption. Where does one start making corrections? If you want any service anywhere, you will pay legal and illegal fees for it. Let the vicious circle continue until we end up in collective self-destruction. The councilors' demand is part of the vicious circle which we have to put up with."

A similar meeting was conducted by every councilor in their various wards and you can be sure the message and the tone were almost the same. Undercover messages were used to bolster up the appeals. Councilors invited trusted agents and gave them commission to 'enlighten' interested candidates the more. The enlightenment consisted in impressing on them the idea that the higher one's offer, the brighter one's chances since every applicant could not expect to be recruited in view of the limited number of vacancies. Councilors collectively asked for one thousand naira but would gratefully have more. The agents were promised a sizeable fraction of the additional offer.

CHAPTER III

'Tim Kom' jingled the intercom bell of the telephone in the office of the chairman of Ikpem Local Government Council. It was the secretary ringing.

"Hello, my honourable secretary, good morning."

"Good morning sir, how is business going?"

"I wonder when I became a businessman. I don't think I have the acumen for business."

"Aren't you funny sir, what can be more business than administering a Local Government Area? If you don't know, you are a district governor."

"Thanks a lot for the compliment. I hope I will one day become a state governor". A broad laugh from the secretary.

"I equally hope you are preparing for it. Sir, I wanted to remind you of the meeting with councilors on Thursday. Have the circular letters for it been sent out?"

"I am afraid they haven't. I have almost forgotten it which reminds me; my private secretary took a casual leave for today and tomorrow. I should be grateful if you would do that today. It will be too late tomorrow."

"That's right, hence I chose to remind you of it today. Thursday is only two days away from today. I will do it right away."

The secretary's promise was as reliable as his smartness was admirable. In less than thirty minutes he had dispatched his messenger with copies of circulars enough to go round the councilors. They were to be hand-delivered and signed for by each recipient. The precaution was hardly necessary as councilors had been anticipating the chairman's summons to the meeting.

At eight o'clock on Thursday morning, the chairman rang his secretary to confirm the meeting scheduled for that day. The secretary was just routinely-dusting his heavily padded chair to ensure that his immaculate white lace remained spotless for the meeting, when the telephone on his table buzzed rotundly. In his obsession with the all-important meeting, he lost a link in his memory. He forgot that the intercom device connecting him with the chairman's office had a different sound system. Picking up the receiver, he habitually voiced the happy mood of the morning.

"Good morning sir; I hope it is the chairman speaking."

"No please", rang the feminine voice he very easily recognized and which roused him from his obsession and day dreaming.

"It is your Suzy. I want to remind you of the poor fellow who called on us a couple of nights ago. He was here a few minutes after you left, almost fainting with anxiety. If you propose to look into their applications today, please endeavour to put in some words in his favour for he can't survive failure."

"Enough of that patronage, dear. I reassured him the other day that I would do my best for him. I can't understand the impatience. In our meeting today, we shall appoint a day for interviews. The applications will be treated during the interviews. Tell him, if he is still there, I shouldn't be pestered any more."

The conversation was cut short by the intercom bell.

"Good morning sir, I hope you had enough relaxation last night."

"Thank you! As much as an endless stream of visitors allowed me. I went to bed at 1a.m. when I summoned courage to send out an approaching group. Our people are a difficult lot. If you throw you door wide open, you find that there will be no end to calling. If you shut your door, they will complain of inaccessibility. The best way out is to find accommodation outside this town, then one can visit at week-ends."

"That sounds plausible sir, but the inconvenience of keeping two houses will soon bog you down. You have to draw a line between courtesy and privacy, and make sure there is no spilling over either way otherwise your health will be compromised."

"Thanks for your advice. I will think over a number of options before long. By the way, I wanted to ask about the circulars. I hope they were sent round."

"Yes sir. I made sure every councilor got his copy by insisting that they sign for it. The delivery book has every councilor's signature."

"That's marvelous. I love the spirit, placing duty before anything else. I hope that when I become the state governor you will be promoted to secretary to government and head of services."

"A glorious dream for me sir, thank you."

The meeting had only one agenda: recruitment of teachers for primary schools. Any other topic was treated casually while the more important ones were put off till the next meeting. The chairman's address was brief and to the point.

"My ever-sharp secretary and hard-working councilors, I hope everyone of us knows the purpose of this meeting today. In a not-too-long time from now we are going to conduct a series of interviews for prospective primary school teachers. When we broached this issue about three weeks ago, we agreed on a gratification fee of one thousand naira per candidate. Call it administrative cost or entertainment fee when you will conduct the interviews, people will raise eyebrows. I do not grudge them that; they have a right to moralise over other people's affairs. But I want to ram home a point here. We should not lose our humanity in the process of conducting the interviews. To you and me one thousand naira is a paltry sum of money but to most of the applicants, it is paying through their nose. We should not bleed them white by asking for an additional kobo (dime). I might add that any candidate we consider unsuccessful; must be refunded the one thousand naira."

The chairman of education committee interrupted him at this point.

"Chairman sir, I think if the fee is meant to cover administrative cost, it should not be refunded."

A majority of the councilors had the same opinion but the chairman insisted:

"I vehemently object to that view. Perhaps this point illustrates what I called losing our humanity. How can you rob a candidate of a thousand naira and at the same time refuse to oblige him with a job offer? I am not a party to such a decision. It is either job or refund."

"A second point I want to stress is, this council hall is no venue for family or political vendetta. For us to recruit the right caliber of teachers for our children, we must eschew bias. At one time or another we have had inter-family feuds, political and business rivals or opponents. Their children or relations must not be made revenge victims. Let us teach our so-called opponents that we are capable of forgiving offences. Merit should be foremost in our mind. A candidate who has several credits should definitely have an edge over a run-on-the-mill candidate. Such an ordinary candidate might have a place if we decide to give special consideration for relatively backward localities."

That point attracted another interruption. Councilor Ike asked:

"What exactly do you mean sir, by backward localities? Do you mean remote villages or those with very-few literate people?

"Thank you for that question. I mean both. We have, at least a school in every village in this local government area. Some villages hardly have a trained teacher. If it happens that a candidate shows up from such a village he or she must be recruited, quality of certificate notwithstanding. It will be a sort of encouragement to the people there to send their children to college. On the other hand, most young people today refuse to work in rural areas especially villages without any social attractions. You wouldn't blame them down-right for there are no good houses for them to rent in those places. If one decides to go to work from one's home, transport cost becomes an impediment. In the light of these obstacles, we have to recruit people from remote villages so that they teach in their villages. It will be a good idea also if, in posting, you give first consideration to a candidate's locality. At this point I must admit that I have no more ideas to tender. I shall, therefore, welcome your contributions and perhaps more questions."

The secretary rose. "Sir, in my opinion, your speech, though brief, has covered enough ground for the recruitment exercise. Let us save ourselves the headache of further debate. I think the next matter is to set the date or dates for the interviews."

He seemed to have spoken the mind of everyone, so his contribution was unanimously upheld. Then the chairman resumed his speech in order to sum it up.

"Mr. Chairman of Education Committee, this is the sole responsibility of your committee. Neither I nor my secretary will participate in the interviews. In place of my secretary, the head of Education Unit will be there. I am surprised he has made no contributions so far."

"Sir", replied the young man already gripped by remorse in connection with the one thousand naira fee which, in his opinion, was not only unnecessary but immoral, "I have seen nothing to comment on. Everything has been as it should be. I shall plead that we heed your warning especially as regards asking for extra fees."

The committee chairman took his turn: "Since we are recruiting teachers for immediate deployment, and the current school term ends in a little more than two weeks from today, we have to conclude our assignment before schools resume next term. We cannot finish the interviews in three sittings; therefore I suggest that we interview candidates on Mondays, Wednesday, and Fridays. We may be able to finish it in the second week. Then we do posting in the third week."

That remark concluded the meeting. Before they dispersed, the chairman prayed that God would guide them to do this important job honestly.

Before the councilors left for their respective homes, they retired to Madam Cash Restaurant where they helped themselves to "pepper soup" and beer. As they relished their delicacy, the committee chairman dropped a hint on a topic he thought would be popular with every council member except possibly the chairman. The restaurant was the wrong place for any secret discussion since it was so popular and was patronized by people from all walks of life. The committee chairman therefore, gave an invitation to all his fellow councilors: "I would love to host a get-together for council members in my house tomorrow at six pm. This life is not meant to be slaved out. Once in a while people should relax in a group and enjoy some food and drink."

As if they were anticipating the invitation all took the cue and welcomed the kind gesture. One of them commented:

"This is the beginning of a welcome trend which will remove boredom and tedium from hum-drum council meetings."

The get-together turned out to be a formal meeting short of recorded discussions. As the happy-go-lucky company munched the fried pieces of meat offered to them, the host councilor chipped in the bon mot: "Yesterday we were treated to a mélange of excellent language and moralizing."

Councilor Ebere took it up from there: "If I am not being harsh, I believe that the chairman exhibited hypocrisy and selfishness. In his words, asking for extra money from applicants is bleeding them white. Good enough for pulpit sermonizing. How many times has he applied financial prudence in executing his function?"

Everybody threw in his voice and there was a confused tirade of recrimination. The sum total of the whole effusion was that the chairman would have the lion's share of the so-called administrative charge, hence he ruled against extra demand. What about his imaginary and inflated contracts? What about the wrong invoicing of purchases which his treasurer always does with his blessing? These practices do not incite concern for the common man whose tax is being misappropriated.

When all had given vent to their pent-up emotion, the host gathered up loose ends thus: "In spite of the chairman's self-righteous admonition, we are not going to have that "Father Christmas" ("Santa Claus") affair. Poor as some of the applicants seem, many are prepared to dish out two thousand naira in order to be employed. One aspect of his speech I regard with sympathy is the special consideration for backward villages. I believe that if we comply in that area we shall have enough cover for any aberration we might be guilty of. Another safeguard is to accept exceptionally good certificate with little ado. We shall play safe by avoiding commitment in these extremes."

Much as they would cherish regular turns in hosting the salve of a get-together, none offered to take the next turn. Perhaps that had better wait and soothe

the conscience after the suppressed self-indictment which would characterize the interviews. Meanwhile clandestine lobbying went on. Beer and whisky changed hands between candidates and their councilors. Some female candidates found it less exacting and perhaps more committing to their patrons to offer themselves. A handful made the erotic overture to the head of education unit. Initially he regarded such bargain as no less dirty than mean. What if after the exploitation one failed to get the job? As he kept searching his Christian conscience, more glamorous girls offered themselves. He succumbed a few times and henceforth found himself unable to resist such invitations.

He returned to his sitting room after one of the escapades overwhelmed with guilt. "What role am I going to play in this affair other than post the candidates declared successful by councilors. Why do I allow myself to be drawn into this mess? Some of these councilors are disguised illiterates who have no reputation or refinement to protect. I have the advantage of a liberal education and exposure to enlightened circles. Above all, I am a professional teacher. Suppose I go back to the classroom after my tenure in this office, what moral lesson can I impart to my pupils with my conscience so mortgaged"? The retreat saved him more commitment and earned him respect from the candidates who failed to seduce him.

Councilor Oforma had an early morning visitor. It was Mr. Ibemere whose son was a contestant in the race for employment. He arrived earlier than Mr. Oforma's usual rising time and so had to wait on the long chair pinned to the floor of the sit-out, after knocking for a few minutes without response from inside. Later a frail boy came round from the back of the house and asked who he wanted to see.

"Councilor Oforma of course. I hope he is in."

"He is still in bed."

"Big free man!" Imagine me sleeping till 5.30 let alone 7 o'clock. When does he rise?"

"He is awake but does not receive visitors till after his breakfast".

"Kindly inform him that Mr. Ibemere is waiting to see him. Let him be aware of my presence. Perhaps he will relax protocol."

"I wouldn't do that. It is contrary to my orders. He heard your knocking. Surely he will be around to attend to you before 8.30."

Ibemere whispered to himself. "If I had known he was a late riser, I would have tapped my palm trees before coming. I feared I would miss him". As he was besieged by impatience he thought of a possible alternative if he failed to evoke sympathy. This exigency had taught him a lesson. Perhaps for the first time in his life, he had realized that very few people were prepared to part with their money unless there was collateral security. Everybody denied having enough money to spare but if land or any other valuable property was pledged, money came out from nowhere.

When sitting became boring he began to stroll round the big compound, observing the flowers that wreathed the house without appreciating their beauty. "Such a big farmland lost to flowers?" he wondered. "A lot of crops could be raised here every year". After a few mirthless rounds, he saw the main door to Mr Oforma's house open. Shoving and stamping his feet on the coarse door mat, he clapped his hands and waited to be ushered in.

"Come in Mr Ibemere. I am sorry you have been waiting. It is my custom not to see visitors before my breakfast otherwise I will miss it that day. Visitors come in a steady stream. Watch and see what happens now. Everyone wants his problems solved instantly. None would understand your explanation or difficulty. It is the same experience everyday, so I decided to stuff myself with food to make sure I stand the strain. Kiran, find me a kola nut."

Having waited so long and fearing that other activities of his would be belated or abandoned completely, he did not go the full length of kola ceremony. He said a very short prayer and broke it.

Kola over, he went straight to his mission. "Councilor sir, you will have realized I never was here since your successful election. I am always in the bush, setting traps, tending to my crops or looking round for ripe palm fruits. We who never went to school have to toil to keep our family going. I am here this morning to make a request and I hope you wouldn't fail me. My first son, as you know, is one of those seeking employment into the teaching profession. I know you have been expecting me to hand in the required fee. I have been trying unsuccessfully to raise the money. Nobody seems to have any kobo to spare. I cannot assess anybody's wealth but I know that some people are more buoyant than others. I should be grateful if you would lend me one thousand five hundred naira, repayable in six month's time."

"Thank you Mr. Ibemere for classing me among the wealthy in the village. I would have lent you the money unconditionally in recognition of your simple honesty and industry but I have committed all the money at hand to my business. I paid seventy thousand naira only yesterday to the brewery for beer supply which I expect next week. My provision store has just been replenished. My store assistant went to Onitsha last week. I am sorry I cannot help you but I have to stress that you must not let the chance slip from your son. He has good results but the Council fee is a must."

"Certainly it will slip", returned Mr Ibemere dejectedly. "I cannot convert myself to money and I hardly have anything to sell. A couple of goats wouldn't fetch enough money. I will go home and console Inno to wait for another chance."

Councilor Oforma read desperation on his face and resolved to edge him on a little more. "You said you have nothing to sell? Don't you have land?"

"I have enough land to sell but my children will blame me seriously in future. My father never sold any."

"That was why he never sent you to school. To him land was a priority instead of your schooling. If you sell land to bolster your children's education, it is not bad. You would be ensuring a bright future for them. I believe that if not the youthful frivolity, he will be able to muster enough resources, in combination with your own effort, to send the younger ones to college and even to university. Land is no longer a scarce commodity. If you have money, you can buy the whole of this local government area. Do you know what your children will become in future?"

"Councilor, there is much sense in what you are saying. I never reasoned like that. I have always upheld my late father's line of thinking. I shall have to pledge some piece of land which my children can redeem when they begin to earn money."

"That will help but you will have easy patronage if you want to make an outright sale. I would have been interested if I had not invested my money in business but I know one or two people who would provide spot cash if you want to sell the land."

"I will think over it. Inno must know about it before I sell it."

Let me know what you decide to do, and make sure Inno doesn't lose this chance."

As was expected, Ibemere was back at councilor Oforma's house three days later. He had a piece of land measuring more than four plots which he was prepared to dispose of, but since it was outright sale, he was asking for three thousand naira instead of one thousand five hundred. Councilor Oforma pouted his lips in the most uninterested manner.

"I told my friends your target. I am not sure they will be prepared to exceed that. In any case come back tomorrow evening. I will contact them before you return here."

Assuming a very sympathetic posture, he recalled Mr Ibemere before he crossed his gate. "In case they refuse to pay three thousand naira, what offer will be acceptable to you? In your situation you have little choice. I advise that you regard your son's employment as priceless and worthy of any sacrifice, if one can rightly call selling one's property to stave off some problem sacrifice."

Although Ibemere had not sold any piece of land before he had heard people quote how much they sold, or paid for a plot of land. He was convinced beyond doubt that his desperate situation was apt for exploitation and that his councilor would love to cash in on such a state of affairs, but his host's remark on his first visit: "You have little choice," could not be more true. He hesitated a little, then as if he had choking cough he managed to say: "I will knock off five hundred naira."

"That's fair enough Mr Ibemere. I must get an interested buyer before you come again."

The story and gossips prevailing in the local government area had almost the same content and pattern. Councilors encouraged the indigent parents of applicants to sell their land and household property, and they (councilors) were invariably the buyers. Where there was no property to sell, the needy guardians were goaded on to borrow money at high interest rates. There was always a go-between who simulated the lender but eventually when agreements were written, councilors surfaced as ambivalent sureties to protect the borrower against usury, and the lender against default in repayment. The stinking scandal was topical in any gathering. The influential *Independent paper*, the champion of the oppressed and the mouth-piece of the upright minority, featured it in its editorial. Not wanting to whip up popular sentiment on the basis of uncorroborated rumour, the affected underdogs being unprepared to tell on their councilors, the paper merely made a general appeal to the "sense of justice of the councilors" and the evanescence of earthly wealth.

The interview did not last as long as expected. Every member of the council, from chairman and his secretary to canversers for contracts, had a protégé among the candidates. Such clients were equipped with short notes designating them "my candidate". Councilors' candidates were asked no questions except where they would like to be posted to. They were dismissed after their credentials had been perfunctorily passed round. Unequipped candidates bore the full weight of the interview. Every councilor tried to exercise his authority. Some of their questions were more inane than irrelevant. The head of Education unit who was brought in to ask professional questions felt frustrated and redundant. He found cover in voluntary dizziness. "I have been feeling out of sorts for few days now. I need to relax in bed. Kindly let me off. I shall come round again the next day if I improve, otherwise I shall not object to your going ahead without me. There is nothing requiring expertise in this type of interview."

With that he disappeared and never rejoined them, and they never missed him.

At home he thrilled his wife with recounting his experience in the council hall, adding: "Poverty and illiteracy are terrible social evils. With a little more literacy the councilors would have realized their ludicrous display of brazen inferiority complex."

CHAPTER IV

Although very slow to make public their grievances some of the dispossessed and cheated citizens took their pastors into confidence, not with the intention of staining their councilors' reputation but to liberate their conscience which was ensnared by fear of complicity in the double-edged sword called bribery. One of the priests so confided in was incensed with a gust of remorse by proxy. He was equally assailed by consciousness of the reality that some of the councilors so castigated were the highest offertory donors and the financial pillars of his church, yet the urge to expose evil and thus deter intending perpetrators waxed to a point of turbulent wave. How would he overlook such bare-faced swindle when in the same church he condemned traditional rulers who made chiefs of notorious cheats? Having resolved to take the bull by the horn, he scheduled the next Sunday service for a time a majority of his parishioners would find most convenient to put up appearance.

The service was at its best; hymns were well chosen and superbly rendered, probably designed to prepare the emotions of the targets to swallow the unexpected bitter pill. Homily time arrived and the priest mounted the pulpit. The congregation at once noticed a sudden switch from a frolicsome to a melancholy visage.

"My dear brethren", he started, today is a unique Sunday; unique in the sense that the theme of the gospel is the greatest commandment – love. A lot has been written on love; people have conceived love in various concepts; many atrocious acts have been justified under the umbrella of love but the only true guide is the Bible. What does the Bible say about love? It starts by giving us the boundaries of love; you must love your God with your whole heart, your whole mind and strength; you must love your neighbour as yourself. No one here needs to be told why he should love God. If not for anything, you are alive and healthy, hence you are here now listening to me. How much bribe did you give God to save your life today? If any of you did, in any way, influence God's decision, let him speak out."

"Why does God ask us to love our neighbour as ourselves? In my prudish opinion, it is because, firstly we are created in his image and likeness. In other words, we are like God himself. Secondly we are all children of God and we have a common ancestry on earth. Therefore we are brothers and sisters no matter our colour, race or creed. In 1 Corinthians 13, St Paul spells out the characteristics of love: it is always patient and kind; it is never jealous; it does not take offence etc. Christ said in one of his lessons on charity: "If you do a favour to one of the brethren, you do it to me. In good homes, brothers and sisters eat food in common, share joys and sorrows. They never hate one another. In our broad home, the earth, "it should be the same."

"We, as individuals, are like the biblical farm. God the good farmer planted in us at birth the virtues of faith, hope and charity, but the enemy, Satan planted vices the chief of which is selfishness, the antithesis of love. This vice makes us love ourselves alone, thus divesting us of the inclination to put other people's welfare into consideration. Excessive devotion to oneself deadens one's sense of justice; it impairs judgment; it extols self-glorification and nurtures insensibility to our neighbours' plight. This vice manifests itself in many ways. When we impassionately demand and exact bribes from people requiring our services, services for which we are duly remunerated; when we unfeelingly wrench unjustifiable rewards from people who have to impoverish themselves in order to satisfy our demand for services yet to be rendered; when we close our ears to heart-dissolving pleadings and our eyes to the tears that gild the coins we grab from them, then we have enthroned for ourselves the twin deities of greed and selfishness". He paused and surveyed the congregation mischievously.

"Who among us in the public service is a heathen? Do we really have heathens in our country today? We are in essence, either Christians or Muslims who have shared beliefs about morality and immorality, decency and indecency, public spiritedness and selfishness. Are all these beliefs, my dear brethren, merely window dressing? Before God every omission or evil commission must be accounted for. Every ill-gotten good must be restored to the rightful owner before we have forgiveness for it, and that restitution must be made while we are alive here on earth. In Matthew chapter sixteen verses twenty four to twenty-six, Christ asks; What does it profit a man if he gains the whole world and suffers the loss of his soul? In Luke chapter twelve verses fifteen to twenty-one, Christ tells us the story of the rich man who amassed wealth for himself as many of us are doing today, and God terminated his life at the point he had prepared his mind to enjoy his wealth. The same fate could befall some of us who increase the plight of the poor to make themselves richer. One sad reality which seems to escape our vision is the enormity of eternity. We can enjoy our wealth for two hundred years on earth but for how long are we going to suffer the torments of hell fire? Forever and ever. Isn't that dreadful? Isn't it terrifying? The members of my church who deepen the wounds of poverty on their neighbours cannot claim to love their neighbours as themselves."

At this point the congregation had difficulty suppressing the urge to react but since, by tradition, the homily is never interrupted with questioning or comments, the spontaneous uneasiness found expression in a general murmur that emanated from every corner of the church. The priest allowed the murmur to burn itself out although its brevity was secured by church wardens.

As the murmuring prevailed, one of the councilors suffered a sudden quivering of his lips. This was precipitated by internal commotion. Should he stand up there and then, make public confessions and ask for forgiveness? Should he maintain his calm and make private restitution in kind thereafter? He was a study in confusion. Although he managed to get the situation under control, his conscience remained unsettled throughout the remaining part of the service.

The Priest wisely decided to quit the stage "while the ovation was loudest". His aim had been achieved. He had touched the hearts of his hearers. So as soon as the murmuring died down, he said:

"Let our conscience be our judge", and left the pulpit. The homily remained the talk in town for several days.

As Mr. Ijeoma, a civil servant was driving home after service, a friend of his in the car remarked: "The priest seems to have had a briefing on the goings-on in the council and civil service in this state. How I wish he preached this to the gathering of workers in the state ministries."

"What do you think that will achieve?" returning Mr. Ijeoma. "Isn't it the same workers who attend services here and there?"

"Yes, but do you think all pastors have enough courage to delve into such a controversial issue as bribery?"

"Well, you can believe what you like but I know that unless one makes up one's mind to give up bribery, no amount of preaching will move him to do so."

"Much to the contrary, sir; being able to resolve against it is a result of the constant reminders by priests. Left alone we would convince ourselves that the wrong thing was right, provided we derived pleasure or gain from it. Those who do not see taking bribes as evil have worked religion out of their system. As far as they are concerned, religion stands between them and the achievement of their earthly goals."

Mr. Ijeoma chose to stop the parley at that point. He concluded: "The priest rounded off the homily appropriately, let our conscience be our judge. Let us therefore leave the matter to individual conscience. We have other more pressing issues to discuss."

The trouble with rumours is the speed of their spread coupled with general indifference about authentication. Peddlers rather touch them up intentionally to work up people's emotion. The Ikpem local government floundering in the teacher recruitment exercise, and the priest's castigation that seemed to open the sluice-gate of criticism portrayed the chairman of that local government in worse light than he deserved. Believing all sorts of crimes leveled against him became more charitable than reasonable. Who would doubt such avarice when he was building mansions in his home town and several urban areas? How many of such property had he before he became chairman?

Dr. Ume had been a very close associate of the chairman right from their secondary school days when they were inmates of one boarding house. Pursuing divergent disciplines in universities outside theirs had not very significantly widened the social gulf between them. Dr. Ume could still vouch for the honesty and humanness of Mr Igbokwe who, in his opinion, was the most just and most respected prefect in his school, a prefect whose decision was always upheld by the principal for he never allowed personal or group sentiment to get the better of him. In the circumstances he found it difficult to reconcile those rumours with his friend's delightful character. He had made two unsuccessful attempts to get him on the phone. Then he decided to pay him an unscheduled visit at his office. At the reception room, he found a crowd wanting to see the chairman. He would jump the queue. "Good morning lady, can I see the chairman?"

"Yes sir, but you can't go in now. There is a visitor in his office and all these people want to see him. You have to fill out this form", and she offered him a form.

"Never mind", replied the doctor politely. "Just peep in and tell him doctor Ume is around."

"Sir, I am afraid I can't do that. I have strict orders not to let people in without going through the formality of filling out forms".

"Just disobey the protocol today", he insisted firmly. "I will explain all to the chairman and take the blame."

"He will not scold me while you are here. It might cost me my job". "I didn't know your job was at stake-but if he takes that extreme measure..."

As he was saying that, the attention bell beside the chairman's table rattled. She rushed into the office, ignoring the doctor.

"Please get me file NP/L/1050 and tell all waiting that I can't see anybody else until 2 o'clock. I have to dispose of this today."

"Yes sir", and, as she was about turning round, she said, "one Dr Ume has been pestering me to let him in"

"But I didn't see his form among the lot."

"No, he refused to fill out the form, insisting that I should simply mention his name to you".

"My goodness, let him in at once."

On emerging she stared at the doctor guiltily.

"Doctor sir, the chairman wants you in."

He threw the door open with a firm pressure on the larch and banged it behind him.

"Hello Doc, how are you getting on with pressure of work at the hospital? It is wonderful you have time to say hello to an old acquaintance, and during office hours for the matter. Please sit down"

"Doing well, thank you. Doc, this is Chief Awa, the Omereoha I of Amazu. He is one of our reliable contractors. He has called several times without seeing me. I want his matter settled today. Chief, this is Dr. Ume of the general hospital here, a good friend and school mate."

"It is a privilege meeting you, Chief" subscribed the doctor, proffering his hand for a warm shake.

"Thank you Doc; it is a pleasure. How is work going on?" "We are doing all we can under the difficult situation. I managed to wriggle out of entanglement with numerous patients". Switching back to the chairman, he said, "John, I would have loved to have a frank chat with you but I can see it's most inconvenient now. Since this week I have rung your office two times but the bogy of "line engaged" intercepted me. When shall we make it then?"

"Thank you Doc for showing such kind consideration. Just one minute". He flipped through the leaves of his desk diary for a few seconds. Looking up, he remarked:

"Visitors literally run shifts here. If you don't mind, let us meet at my residence on Friday at 5.p.m."

The doctor had no diary but he had his work schedule in his head. Looking pensively into the blank space he replied: "That day will do. My evening ward round that day comes on between 4 and 5 p.m. I shall bring it forward so as to be free by 4.30 p.m. Make sure you don't propose any other engagement for that hour. I will attend to some private patients at 7 p.m."

"I shall endeavour not to."

"Thank you, John; Bye Chief".

As they were sorting things out, the receptionist slipped in; placed the ordered file at the right hand side of the chairman and disappeared unnoticed. Reclining back at his chair, he glanced at his watch and it was half past twelve. "Oh my gosh, time really flies! Where is the daughter of a bitch I asked to get me a file?" Just as he wanted to press the bell trigger, he cast his eyes to the right and saw the file.

"Dear, I didn't see her bring the file. Is she a spirit?"

"No, threw in Chief." "You know our attention was taken by the doctor. She must have come in while we were conversing."

"You see why people accuse us of discrimination. To me nobody is less a human being. I would sooner attend to the so-called low class than my coffee break but I can't throw you out in order to see other people most of whom have very trivial matters my secretary can handle."

"Chairman, you are doing well. You can't attend to a hundred people in one day. Don't mind what they say. No one man can satisfy a legion."

"I wish many people understood our uneasy position as you do. Now back to business. How many tipper loads of gravel have you delivered so far?"

"Ten, Chairman."

"Ten in one week? Do you really intend to execute this contract? You have two tipper trucks. One would expect you to have done with dumping concrete."

"Yes Chairman, I have tipper trucks but I have no gravel dump neither do I do the excavation myself. In the recent past, the dealer's price has almost doubled. But for the regard I have for your person, I would not have exceeded two trips. I am wondering how we can get on."

"I regret the astronomical rise but what do you except me to do? Perhaps revaluing." You needn't mention that. The next day, arm-chair critics will blare it into everybody's ear that the chairman has singled-handed revalued a contract in order to illegally enrich himself. We have to stick strictly to the terms of the agreement, am afraid."

"That would be nothing short of spelling my economic doom. My survival depends entirely on contracts and there is always provision for revaluation to suit the prevailing economic climate."

"Yes but one has to surrender oneself to the political current else he will encounter a tragic storm. Believe it or not, my election to this post cost me about one million naira. If I don't stay out my tenure, I will never recover my money. I have no stomach for impeachment or probe, whatever you call it".

"Who will impeach you? We are the community leaders. Perhaps you under-rate our influence. I can lead a delegation to the governor to plead your case. Isn't the governor an ordinary human being? Some of us can get closer to him than you can imagine."

"If we must revalue it, councilors and the accounts head that will effect payment will know about it.

Then the vicious circle of lobbying continues thus diminishing your overall profit. Couldn't you speed up action on the gravel supply in order to beat doubling the price?"

"I cannot guarantee the roadworthiness of old tipper trucks. Anyone of them can break down any time, more so with the increased pressure of running several times a day. But chairman there is a way out". He drew his chair nearer the chairman's table and lowered his voice.

"I have an easy way out. You will simply approve on paper an increased number of gravel loads. Neither the councilors nor the accounts head will suspect it. The explanation is simple: it has been discovered early enough that instead of twenty tipper loads, thirty will meet the requirements. Lowering his voice a little more, he said: "The council will pay for thirty loads at the current rate while, in fact, only twenty loads are supplied. Whatever is surplus over and above will be shared between us in an equitable proportion."

Taking a hard look at the chief, Mr Chairman said despondently, "this sounds ingenious but who will guarantee its secrecy?"

"You wouldn't expect me to be so mean as to divulge the secret of my success as a contractor. I would rather die than live to face the media and the hungry citizens of this local government area."

"All right, make sure delivery is completed by the middle of next week."

Mr Chairman had just got up from siesta and was reclining on a surplus settee, looking a little stupefied by an over-dose of sleep. A few seconds later, he heard a gentle revving of a car engine right inside his yard, and the revving died almost instantly. Before he heaved his bulk to ascertain who the visitor was, Dr Ume was already at the door.

"Hello Doc", he was now wide awake, "you are still a black whiteman, your association with rustic folk notwithstanding. You wouldn't come a minute later than 5 o'clock."

"Thank you John, habits die hard. Many people who have had appointment with me won't say much that is complimentary about me. They have always had disappointment for I wouldn't allow one engagement to encroach on the other. Once your time is up, I dismiss you unceremoniously for I know that a little delay can make a lot of regrettable difference. Well, I hope you had some time to yourself today."

"Time to myself indeed. You had better say time to have mid-day coffee. That office is hell short of an unimagined degree of physical heat. Nevertheless the heat often generated by an overwrought brain compares favourably with the idea of hell we were given in our primary school days."

"John, your sense of humour remains resourceful. I think only children will pity your painted plight. An adult wouldn't be one if he didn't wonder why you remain there in spite of the horror, and would go to any length to be re-elected at the expiration of your tenure of office. However, accept my sympathy for, in spite of every thing, every public office has its own unique type of problem."

"What would you taste, Doc? Beer, champagne or whisky?"

"Thanks a lot. I would rather prefer our discussion took precedence over refreshment. I don't have much time to spare. I will go straight to the point. I must confess, I admire your capacity for stomaching revolting rumours. If I heard half as much about my own office, I would have either relinquished my post or resorted to law suits. I like to believe that you were neither involved in, nor did you cover up, the mess being widely spread with regard to the recruitment of staff for primary schools in this local government area. I have had no reason yet to lose confidence in your fair-mindedness in treating the public. If previous experiences are anything to go by these hectic days, one would stake anything in defence of your moral probity. Our colonial school principals trusted you among the few blacks they could afford to credit with honesty and reliability. Perhaps your councilors have used your name as a cover for their contemptible extortion from the poor teachers they have just recruited. Your council has everything but merit and praise for it."

Mr. Igbokwe's reaction, though fraught with disbelief, elicited sympathy from Dr. Ume who had expected an explanation in defence of the chairman's integrity but instead saw surprise on his face. Could he pretend not to have heard the rumour, even the admonitory sermon which was now a household discussion in the local government area?

"I am not kidding you Doc; I never heard a comment about the council since the recruitment exercise was concluded. I wouldn't pretend, though, that the council wasn't the target of unpalatable comments since councilors and local government councils have the stigma of taking bribes real and imagined."

"I am dumb-founded Mr. Igbokwe. If I had any reason to reconsider my appraisal of you, I would call you a downright liar right here now. Although apparently you have given up formal practice of religion, I would sooner accept the delusion that white is black than I would countenance your denial of ever hearing anything about the recruitment bungling, even the aftermath of a sermon which has cast a pall, so to speak, over the length and breath of the local government area."

"What sermon, Doc? Surely you wouldn't expect me to discuss trifles with people in a society riddled with rumour mongering and running down of envied personalities."

"Let me believe that the powers usually wielded by chairman of local governments have not intoxicated you to the degree of refusal to draw a line between propriety and meanness which is a common malady of people at the helm of affairs in our continent. Trusting your sincerity then, I would advise you to forget the sermon ignorance of which is better salve for your physical and moral health than being conversant with it. I plead that you do not regard my forthrightness as complicity in falsely accusing you of crimes. You hardly need to be told that I will defend you anywhere your good name is being smeared. It is no longer a secret that your councilors collected more than a thousand naira from each of the scraggy and famished parents of the newly recruited primary school teachers in the local government. That offence, if people still regard bribery as an offence in this country, would appear a lot more pardonable if the unpatriotic councilors did not in a devilishly subtle manner, dispossess indigent villagers of their land and other valuable belongings."

As the doctor reeled off the ignoble techniques the councilors degenerated to in order to ensure their "pound of flesh", his misgiving about the chairman's crass ignorance of the whole thing, as reflected in his mood and gestures deepened to a point of open defiance but he patiently bottled up the emotion.

Mr Igbokwe seemed to have got the message in the doctor's mind and eyes. Surrendering to self-indictment, he succumbed to a posture of pleading.

"Believe me Doc, I didn't know of any collections from parents and relations of the recruits let alone dispossessing them of land and other valuables. However, if I had heard about it I wouldn't have been able to prevent it. You know the mentality of our people. A desperate person can go to any length. Even those so deprived and impoverished would deny it in a law court for fear of repercussions on the desperate job-seekers. On the other hand, councilors are fellow adults. I can only appeal to their sense of justice and moral cleanliness. I have no authority or means of enforcing any law against alleged bribery which would never be confirmed or corroborated. I can see you are glancing at your watch; we have a lot to talk over as regards the corruption that pervades our country. Much as I roundly condemn the action of councilors I should not like the council to be made the sacrificial lamb in a country where it is more admirable to display ill-gotten wealth than die in honest poverty."

Yes, your observation is right. I must be leaving now. We can make time in the near future to have an uninhibited debate on it."

Doc, don't forget that you have taken nothing. Uche, bring him drinks."

"Since you bother so much, I will have only a bottle of malt."

CHAPTER V

Once more the council premises was a centre of gravitation for the prospective teachers. Information had been leaked to some of them that their posting had been completed and that they would soon be getting letters. The posting had taken so long that for some of them patience was running out. The surging into education secretary's Office became such a nuisance that he spoke out in exasperation: "Who invited you? Who told you that your posting is ready? Your councilor friends who leaked the information to you wouldn't have the honesty to tell you that they delayed the posting with unnecessary interference. Almost all of you are councilors' candidates. Go to them and find out where you are posted for they made the dictation. Let nobody protest to me when you know your station. I did what I was ordered to do."

Back in his office after dispersing the inquisitive rabble, he saw a letter from an unfamiliar office lying on his table. The first impulse was to throw it aside as one of those letters of dictation that got on his nerves but since the writer's name was not written at the back of the envelope, instead the stamp of the Ministry of Works and Transport was neatly pressed at the bottom left-hand corner of the envelope, he decided to open it for fear of neglecting a call for duty in a fit of anger. The letter ran thus:

My dear Education Secretary,

I should be grateful if you would appreciate the pressure under which I write this letter. I am Mr. Ijemere, permanent secretary in the Ministry of Works and Transport. I happen to be related to one of the new recruits for primary schools in your local government area. Assuming that you will have a free hand in the posting of the new teachers, I make bold to request a favour which I hope you will grant me. The candidate in question is Miss Chinyere Nwobodo from Okosi town.

I have arranged evening classes for her in the state capital aimed at her attempting the Joint Admission Matriculation Board (JAMB) test this year to enter university. In consideration of this plan, therefore, it would do her a world of good if she is posted to one of the schools on the major road to the state capital, just to facilitate her movement to and fro.

I hope I have not bothered you too much. Trusting in your co-operation, I wish you God's guidance in the execution of your onerous duty. I wouldn't like to make any promises yet but I shall surely show gratitude.

Thanks,

Yours sincerely,

W. Ijemere.

"Free hand indeed", he complained aloud. Can one ever be allowed to do one's duty the way one thinks best in this God ...... damned country of ours? People must make you feel their influence while job-seekers must make you know they have important connections. How many of this type of letter have I received since after the interview? All have a similar content. By the way how many schools have we on the all-important major road? Surely the chairman's pre-interview address fell on deaf ears. If I oblige all these disinterested self-appointed patrons, aren't we going to run into difficulty trying to staff remote schools? It would be shortsightedly presumptuous to believe that more letters of this nature wouldn't be received. How does one get along with one's hands so tied? The chairman who would have helped to arrest the situation is the first culprit."

For about half an hour the secretary was musing. As he was ruminating over the foibles of his fellow men, a hot shaft of guilt thawed the forming icicles of contempt for all who tried to rob him of initiative in the execution of his duty. He had posted some of the female candidates who had made his resolve spineless to points easily accessible to him, justifying his action with the plea that he never unduly exploited anybody neither did he have a share of the interview fees enjoyed by the councilors.

Back at home after the ordeal of moral assessment of himself and fellow public officers, he thought of getting relief by sharing the safe parts of his experiences with his wife.

"Juli, in less than a week from today, you will be relieved of much of the load of controlling over a hundred pupils. The posting of new teachers has been completed and letters will soon be dispatched to the recruited teachers."

"Welcome news at last. My voice has virtually grown hoarse with shouting. To be candid, I have practically taught nothing this term. With Mrs. Imo gone on maternity leave my class swelled to almost one hundred and fifty. Every minute I am busy either putting down chaotic noise or separating fighting pairs."

"You have taught a lot dear. Controlling the mob you have is the first step to effective teaching. You cannot impart knowledge in a bedlam. When they realize the need to listen to the teacher, then formal teaching can take shape.

"Darling I would have forgotten a message. Mrs. Ebere of Central School stopped over at my school on her way to your office. I discouraged her coming to see you as that would be intolerable tampering with your time and concentration."

"She must be coming to request teachers. I know her school was grossly understaffed. I am sending her four teachers."

"Yes but she would have liked to stress that you send more male teachers. Of the staff of twenty-two, only three are male, all too old to be games master".

As his wife said that, his mind was pricked. That school received one of his pet female recruits and some other councilor's candidates. In fact he sent no male teacher there.

"I cannot create male teachers. The teaching profession is fast becoming a female affair at primary school level in this state in particular. Eighty percent of the recruits are women. Besides, experience has shown that men are more tolerant of posting into non-urban areas. Some have bicycles and are prepared to ride considerable distances to their schools. I am sorry I can't send her any male teacher this academic year. She should make do with what she has. Women can train sports boys and girls, cant they?"

"Well, I have delivered her message. Now that the posting is over and perhaps the embargo on head teachers visit to your office is lifted, she might be there next week. You will convince and appease her. She seemed to be bent on getting at least one young male teacher. I am not holding brief for her but I see her problem."

"Even a blind man can see her problem if you really call it a problem but I am afraid the practical solution is not imminent. Better still, she could save herself a lot of trouble by temporarily scrapping male-dominated games like football. She might have had better consideration if undue influences were not thrust on me. Nearly all prominent civil servants in this state have female candidates among the new recruits who must be posted to "convenient places."

"O dear, how I wish you didn't pander to their devilish inclination."

"Darling, I take strong exception to the word pander. You don't mean I made myself an obsequious servant to my fellow public servants."

"Sorry dear if that hurts. I mean you should not have gratified their lustful designs. Most men are unfair to their wives. They line up concubines at places of call. Of course they have the usual excuse of leaving office late for pressure of work or having departmental meetings till late in the evening, and this occurs at regular intervals."

"You women are suspicious by nature. You believe the story of working till late hours in the office is a ruse for calling at girlfriends' houses. What prevents a man from taking a girl-friend to a hotel during office hours? You think every man has time for such frivolity and yet takes care of the family."

That is not a strong point. Family responsibilities are not a hindrance to anyone who has formed the dirty habit. What about the invisible income of most civil servants some of which is several times the basic salary of the recipient?"

"That is wonderful. No affair of mine is hidden from you. How much is my invisible income?"

"You simply don't want it. Your position is suspicious for it."

"Well forget that. Those who made special appeals for posting some teachers to specified places have blood relationship with their protégés. You know the extended family system in our society has a lot of tentacles."

"Blood relationship indeed. Who is deceiving whom?" You believe women are daft. Surely we are, for believing your plausible stories always and accepting to date married men who aren't much younger than our own fathers."

"Not all women are fortunate enough to have husbands, and some husbands are hard put to satisfying their wives' material taste."

"Then they should take to prostitution and lose the esteem a good number of married women should enjoy from men."

"This rationalization deserves to be widespread. Do you mind the chairman arranging a seminar for women in the local government area to be addressed by you and a few other selected women? That will bring you to the limelight in the local government area."

"I am sick of publicity. You never know what women go through. I have had enough of passes from men I thought were respectable."

"That is bad enough anyway. Men are always placed on the defensive side. Would you ever believe that some women make passes at men?"

"Although one couldn't rule that out in these days of insatiable needs, it sounds silly and unimaginable to me. What pride do we have left if we should beg men to make fun of us?"

"Let us leave these social problems to take care of themselves. That they are universal is typified in marriage, a tenacious social contract. Every married couple has unique problems and knows how to get over them."

"Yes, let's drop it. Believe it or not women must always be on the losing side."

"You make women look unnecessarily pitiable but in reality they enjoy the fruits of man's labour, married or single."

"Thank you for placing women in such a comfortable background. I wish it was possible to exchange sexes. Excuse me, let me see what my house help is doing. She will burn the rice if she is not directed at every stage", and she left the sitting room.

In the information unit of the state ministry of education, copies of the commissioner's circular letter inviting local government education secretaries to a meeting were being rolled off. The meeting was to take place a little over one month after the new teachers had reported for duty at their various schools. The commissioner, though a very busy man found it very necessary to address the education secretaries himself. It would be more fool hardy than unimaginable for anyone of those invited to be a minute late for the meeting. The circular letter put the opening of the meeting at 10.00am but the conference room of the Ministry of Education was filled to the brim by 9.15am invited and uninvited news hunters had already entered the hall. At 9.55am, the commissioner flanked by the secretary of the State Schools Management Board (SSMB) and chief inspectors of education in the ministry entered the hall. He was greeted by dead silence broken by the creaks of chairs as the audience adjusted themselves to their chairs when be stood up to address them.

"My dear secretaries, or should I call you field officers, I will start this address by relaying the message of His Excellency, the governor of our state. He expressed unreserved gratitude and satisfaction with the business-like execution of a very important assignment. In the same vein, I have to apologize that, owing to the financial stringency which restrains government efforts to make our state number one in education, we are unable to employ more than the stipulated quota. However, I hope we have been able to make a significant thrust into the perennial staff problem in our primary schools. The next thrust, perhaps next financial year, will see victory home."

A spontaneous return of applause with clapping refreshed the commissioner.

"We have recruited the teachers, beginners for that matter, who, besides undergoing a crash program course, have been rendered ineffective by disuse. Whatever remains of the teaching method they learnt will be neutralized by the general apathy of teachers in the school system. The unusual problems and risks, the aftermath of the civil war, which affect every facet of life, dealt a lethal blow to education. Staff quarters have been abandoned to rodents for fear of harassment by men of the underworld; most teachers prefer riding or walking long distances to school to finding accommodation in the vicinity of their schools; more teachers than not are engaged in petty trade and other money-yielding businesses at the expense of writing lesson notes, preparation of lessons and marking of given exercises. The regrettable but often unavoidable delay in paying teacher's salaries tends to lend justification to these lapses in the profession. If really we seriously intend not to create a situation whereby the deadwood in the profession will impart ineptitude to the new comers, if our laudable efforts will not lapse into inanity and be ridiculed by cynical arm-chair critics, and none of you, I hope, will cherish such a situation, then, you field officers, I am afraid, will have to engage in what I would describe as a program of on-the-spot retraining for both old and new teachers, especially the latter. By this I mean a re-intensification of regular inspection to your schools. The visits need not be intimidating or fault-finding; rather they should be corrective in essence. Be prepared to take over lesson teaching from erring or insufficiently informed teachers, simply to demonstrate the right way to handle a lesson and save the pupils ignorance and wrong information."

"As I mentioned earlier, going to school from one's home, irrespective of distance is now a fad. We should therefore expect staff lateness which is a prelude to truancy. I believe none of us whose moral fibre is sensitive will deny the fact that any effort to correct pupil's late-coming habit will be futile unless teachers are first reclaimed. I enjoin that you summon head teachers in your respective local government areas and brief them on the relevant parts of this address. They will introduce time books which will be strictly kept. Persistently defaulting teachers should be given queries copies of which should be sent to you so that you will be able to determine appropriate disciplinary action."

"Bearing in mind the militating financial constraint the state government is grappling with, it is only sensible to balance the increased expenditure the Ministry of Education will have to accommodate with a legitimate pruning exercise. This will affect teachers in primary and secondary schools, ministry and board officials and the non-academic staff of the school system. Dossiers have been designed to update our records of service. Every teacher will have to fill out one as honestly as possible. Based on the records, it will be easy to determine a teacher's retirement date. If we must ensure that the teachers we trained will not rot away in idle waste, we have to retire the serving ones when they are due. At the end of this meeting, you will collect heavy loads of the document from the Chief Inspector's office."

"Lastly, collection of the token fees approved for pupils in the primary school must be meticulously done and rigorously accounted for by head teachers. Getting near our teachers' end financially, so to speak, we can ill-afford to tolerate embezzlement of our scarce funds. Any head teacher who does this, risks outright dismissal; at best, premature forcible retirement."

"At this point, my dear officers, I have to call it a day in order to give attention to other pressing matters in my office. I shall welcome a few questions before I leave the hall."

One journalist asked: "Honourable commissioner, sir, you mentioned collecting of school fees from pupils in the primary school; what do you make of the federal government decree declaring primary schools tuition free throughout the federation? Wouldn't you believe that if the federal government got wind of it, our state would be surcharged?"

"My gentleman, your fear is as genuine as mine but we have no gazette to that effect yet. How can we base such an important policy matter on radio announcement? When the gazette is out, the necessary funds will be made available to offset the increased expenditure I referred to earlier."

A second question from yet another outsider. "Honourable commissioner sir, much as we heave a sigh of relief at the prospect of improved staffing in our primary schools, we are nonplussed to find our secondary schools starved of teachers when hundreds of thousands of graduates and National Certificate of Education (N.C.E.) holders are roaming our streets, some taking to armed robbery and other acts of reprobation. Some have gone to other states to improve their staff quality when the "children of the bride-groom" starve. How do we reconcile this retrograde void with our determination to make our state number one in education?"

"To start with, it is not true that our secondary schools are starved of teachers. Some schools, in fact, have more than their due share of the different cadres of teachers. Our statistics unit has been working round the clock, compiling up-to-date lists of teachers in different schools subject by subject, cadre by cadre. At the end of the exercise, we shall be able to relocate teachers according to need. So we have already embarked on the policy of rationalization. As regards our skilled sons and daughters wallowing in idleness, we deprecate that and would do all we can to remedy the situation. The state government is not to blame in any way. First, there is little federal presence in this state. Consequently, the few state-owned enterprises can not absorb the myriads churned out each year by the tertiary institutions in the country. Secondly, our state has the largest number of secondary and primary schools in the federation. Our staff salary bill is so staggering that a slight increase will trigger off an economic collapse in the state, hence we resort to staff rationalization. As soon as the financial state of the ministry improves, more teachers will be employed."

A third person shot-up his finger. The commissioner announced that that was going to be the last question.

"Sir, it is no longer a secret that the newly engaged teachers were squeezed dry before they were employed. In fact, it was a matter of cash and carry. In the circumstance therefore, how can we be sure that the right candidates were employed? Secondly, wouldn't that experience demoralize the new comers and incline them to other engagements incompatible with the profession? Then we shall have, I should say for want of a better phrase, cut our nose to spite our face."

"Well, we cannot build on allegation or rumour. Assuming it is true, the act is reprehensible. In terms of staff recruitment and general supervision, primary schools are controlled by local government councils. They did the recruitment. We in this ministry merely oversee the running of those schools just to co-ordinate activities. If the wrong people are recruited, they will surely fall out of the system through a system of checks and balances. We cannot allow a handful of people to destroy the edifice that has cost us money and talent to erect."

That last statement attracted protracted applause which saw him off the hall. The audience left the hall in spontaneous groups, discussing different aspects of the address. Those who would not ask questions for fear of risking their jobs or promotion now opened up. One said: "Our state is a place where everyone over-rates his wisdom. Yet we are the loser for it. What gazette are we waiting for which will supersede the federal government decree? Have other states been sent the all-important gazette? My Local Government Area is at the boarder with another state, and because we speak a common language across the boarder, many of our pupils have drifted into the neighbouring state to enjoy free education. Some of the schools in that state are so populous now that they have two sessions when some of our own schools are about to be phased out or merged with others."

"Oh yes" threw in another, "that is to the advantage of the ministry since the need for employment of more teachers won't arise, but they forget that it is poor old parents that are denied the little relief the federal government provided."

Another group took up the retirement bomb-shell. "The idea of retirement seems scaring at first mention but might not be bad by and large", intoned one secretary. "Those who have been long in service without a break will be better off, since they will enjoy handsome gratuity and seventy percent of their terminal salary as their pension."

"That is consoling enough but there are annoying aspects of it. Some of them will die in misery because their benefits will not be approved until they have spent their little savings, if any, processing it. The other side of the story is that, on paper, teachers, ministry and board officials are liable to retirement but, in fact, only teachers will be retired. Board and ministry officials have easy access to their files and they continue swearing to affidavits until they are shown to have started work the very year they were born. The very fellow who will sign your retirement paper – thanks to hair dyes, his hair remains glossy green-might have been your teacher in the primary or post-primary institution. If everybody would quit at the right time, nobody would grudge."

A third person added his protest: "I cannot understand why teachers are treated as the scum of the society in spite of the invaluable role they play in the community. Many practicing teachers who denigrate teaching do not have any inherent antagonism for the profession but they are bitter about the second-rate treatment meted to teachers even by their products who find their way into the civil service."

"That is a very bad omen for the job", the next person continued. "No teacher would like his children to go through the same debasing experience. Perhaps by way of divine reward for their sacrifice, more than ninety percent of their children turn out to be academic stars. If these excellent brains drift from the profession, only half wits will eventually continue teaching as a last resort. You can imagine what educational standards will be when this happens."

The originator of this topic took over". The same vicious circle will continue while the same poor village people will remain the victims. Private schools are springing up here and there. Their staffing is superb because unemployed high callibre manpower is readily available while the conditions for service are excellent, but how many villagers can pay their prohibitive fees? It is the same highly placed civil servants who grow fabulously rich by the stroke of the pen that can afford to send their children there. As far as they are concerned, the so-called qualitative education is a class symbol. Children of poor parentage should be daubed with a scum of literacy which makes them unfit for anything other than menial jobs, while their own class will perpetually replenish the society with professionals and bureaucrats. This society is ripe for land-slide revolution and if it does come, it will be catastrophic for them. People will start the cleaning right from their homes. These class-conscious people do not give a thought to the plight of the poor masses around them. Their blood relations not excluded."

CHAPTER VI

Dr. Ume had been frustrated out of the civil service. Practicing his cherished profession in government hospitals had little thrill for him. The out-of-stock syndrome gave him the creeps. Patients were given prescriptions to go and buy the required medicines from chemists. More often than not, they bought them from quacks who gave them fake or expired drugs ostensibly in consideration for their apparent poverty. Those fortunate enough to get their supply from the hospital hardly receive the prescribed quantity as pilfering of drugs from hospital stores was a normal practice. One father returned his little daughter to the doctor with the same complaint a fortnight after she had exhausted her doses. The doctor was mad with surprise. "Did you give her the full cycle of dosage?"

"Yes", replied the man, saddened with suspicion of wrong prescription.

"How many injections did she receive?"

"Only One."

"Why?" he shouted.

"The nurse said it was all that was prescribed for her."

"What hell of a place where even trained medical professionals toy with human life for petty avarice!"

He sent for the nurse and scolded her sternly before his patients.

The surgical section was an eye-sore. Equipment was antiquated and grossly insufficient. Halfway through an operation one day, the Nigeria Electric and Power Authority cut off electric current. That was a recurrent experience. One of the nurses assisting him ran to the plant house and relayed his order that the stand-by generator be switched on at once. She returned the message that there was no fuel to start the engine. He dropped the scalpel and other surgical instruments he had on the trolley with a terrible clang and stood speechless as if electrocuted. Regaining consciousness he said: "The sooner one gets out of this voluntary prison the better. Everybody is lax. Nothing works unless some dirty naira changes hands. Human life is devalued beyond redemption in this country. This sort of thing never happens anywhere else in the world."

The same day, he gave a month's notice of his resignation. Starting a new hospital in the face of escalating drug and equipment cost was a harrowing experience, yet he was regained by the fact that he was not forced by exigency to resort to unreliable alternatives, neither did he have to wait for orders before doing what he thought was expedient. A good number of the enlightened patients who shared his feelings at the general hospital and sympathized with him, patronized his hospital and recommended it to others who were prepared to pay adequately for thorough treatment. His bills were a clear attestation that he put medical etiquette before financial gain. When it became unavoidable that some of his patients must go for specialist treatment or look for very scarce drugs outside, he recommended hospitals and pharmacies that had some dignity to protect. His staff was a collection of lay missionaries who were constantly reminded of the sacredness of human life, and their duty to work towards saving it at all costs. Protocol was waived with regard to emergency cases. These humanitarian traits of the young hospital gave it unprecedented prominence resulting in accommodation problem for it.

The new commitments notwithstanding, he discovered that he had more time to himself than when he had scheduled duties in the general hospital. The fact that every member of staff knew his duty and did not have to wait to be ordered about obviated unnecessary waste of time.

With settled life, memory performed its duty perfectly. Bewilderment gave way to sobriety, and leisure had a place in his daily routine. At the tennis court several months later, the doctor's new-found recreation venue, the pandora box of recruitment mishandling was tossed up by a club member. Out of sheer courtesy, Dr. Ume feebly defended his friend, well aware that his defence wouldn't make much impact on the biased minds of people who would speak their minds even in the presence of the councilors or their chairman. The most vocal of the critics carried his remark farther afield.

"I began to suspect that the post of chairman of local government council had become a gold mine when medical officers and engineers turned their back to their professions and spent thousands of naira to contest it."

"Isn't that an outrage to such noble professions?" replied another member. "I would have thought that such political posts were for retired public servants, businessmen and lawyers who have enough time for them."

A third person voiced his view: "You see, in this country, every noble ideal is bastardized. In civilized countries, a medical officer, for instance, would not go for a job outside his profession. Doctors regard their profession as sacred, demanding utmost sacrifice which no remuneration can equal. Here, first consideration is given to money."

The businessman in their midst was impelled to voice his feelings about hospital blemishes since the first shot was fired by a medical officer: "Thank you Dr. Ume for making this dispassionate and sincere remark. In general (public) hospitals don't some doctors intentionally dilly-dally in the face of emergency cases until the patients became hopeless whereas the same doctors would forgo leisure in order to attend to such patients in their private hospitals simply because their bills will compensate them for any loss? In the colonial days, white doctors abandoned their meals if there was emergency admission. It is a pet idea to blame whatever goes wrong in this country on the colonial masters. How many of their virtues did we learn? I wonder whether we have anything like medical etiquette in this country today."

In a rejoinder Dr. Ume remarked, "In our next national meeting, one of us should move that in future, any medical officer who abandons his profession in preference for politics should be barred from further practice by the medical association."

Dr. Ume could understand a medical officer seeking entry into the national assembly to forestall selfish politicians relegating the noble profession, but contesting local government council chairmanship was hitting below the belt. Those who do it are best described as mercenary quacks. There and then he decided to take his chairman friend by surprise that evening, if anything, to exorcise from himself the sympathy gilt which had been perturbing his mind since he first heard the scandalous story about his friend's local government council.

He did everything but take his friend unawares. It appeared as if realizing later that Doc discerned guilt in his simulated innocence, he took time to collect materials for his defence. Doctor Ume timed his visit very well. The last batch of his visitors was just moving out of his gate when he arrived.

"Welcome Doc. And congratulations on the rapid growth of your hospital. I learnt it is one of the famous private hospitals in town."

"Thank you chairman. I hope the rumoured prominence will be a reality".

"Sit down, Doc. I hope you are not in a hurry as usual"

"Not at all. I am a bit relieved."

"This time you denied me the courtesy of informing me of this visit before-hand."

"No please, you got it wrong. Formality implies rigidity whereas informality removes encumbrance. I personally associate formality with strict business, so when I feel like being in a relaxed mood, I discard it. I hope you are not expecting more visitors."

"Not at all. If they do come, they may have to come again tomorrow or any other day."

"How are you getting on with council responsibilities?"

"I doubt that I am getting on well. People seem to be more interested in vilifying us than approaching us to get facts clear and make constructive suggestions. One needs to develop very thick skin to remain in the council for more than six months."

"So your skin is thicker now than usual? Guard against hypertension. Such artificial thickness presages it."

"I hope I wouldn't have it, but if it does come, you are always handy."

"Now on a serious note Mr Igbokwe but please, don't accuse me of sliding back to formality at the wrong time. I want to be assured that you were not involved in the very much bandied scandal, and if you were, the degree of involvement so that I can spare myself the trouble of defending a defenseless act. Today at our tennis club, it dominated our conversation. The comments were hard and defamatory."

"Thank you very much for showing so much concern about my personal integrity. You still treasure the experiences of the good old days. My people have a saying that if an accused person owns up, there will be no need for uncalled-for witnessing. With my approval the council collected an application fee of one thousand naira from each interested candidate to meet administrative cost. If councilors on their own made further demands, I did not know about it. As I said the day you asked this question first, even if I knew, I could neither have prevented it nor taken any action against them. That is beyond my powers."

"Mr Igbokwe, I will not spare you embarrassment. If you think I am harsh, you are right but I am bound in honesty to tell you the blunt truth. It was mean of you giving approval to such a debasing demand."

"Doc. that is too harsh."

"Yes, but you were harsher in trampling moral probity."

"To hell with your moral probity. What atrocity have we committed? What facet of public service is free from this debasing demand?"

"You had a name before. Why did you choose to stain it publicity?"

"I was deceiving myself living in a fool's paradise where nobody cares for your good name."

"Don't say that. You can't defend it. Some people still attach importance to their good name. They may be in the minority; it doesn't matter."

"They are found everywhere. Why did you leave the general hospital? Have you forgotten so soon the case of Dr Nna who worked with a conscience to the annoyance of his fellow doctors in the same hospital? His reward for working tirelessly to relieve fellow human beings of pain and suffering was arranging for thieves to snatch his car from him as he was leaving the hospital late. Where is he now?"

"You cannot prove that his fellow doctors arranged for the theft. Even if it could be verified, that was a singular happening. How many cars have been snatched from their owners since then? Who engineered those operations?"

"Moral advocate, reserve your energy for you have a lot to defend. I will give you a litany of incidents in your discipline and department. If they don't suffice, I venture into other departments. How many post-mortem reports are not corruptly influenced? What form does medical examination for candidates seeking admission to educational institutions or prospective employees take in general hospitals today? It is not mean when a doctor gives a certificate of medical fitness or a sick report, obtaining permission to be off duty for some days or weeks without seeing the candidate in question let alone conducting any test, but it is an abomination if a councilor asks for gratification for ensuring the livelihood of an erstwhile idle person. It does not cause public concern if a doctor reports for duty at 10 a.m or much later and, that notwithstanding, engages in private conversation with nurses and other acquaintances for another thirty minutes, ignoring a crowd of patients anxiously expecting treatments. Of course he owes nobody any apology. Is it a wonder that the same plagues are beginning to rear their ugly heads in private hospitals? Isn't it the same breed of doctors and nurses who were infected with indiscipline in general hospitals that man most of these private ones? Now medical lawyer, open your defence."

"I will not defend anybody who errs even if he is my father. These anomalies do happen yet there are still medical personnel who live exemplary lives in their places of work. On the other hand, why should we support the wrong thing morally and practically? Is evil so good that everyone must accept its creed? In this materialistic age when everybody seems to be losing their heads, there must be some who live above board in every community, otherwise we are doomed to collective madness and eventual destruction both here and in eternity."

"I am afraid you will be disappointed. Where do you start your correction? Law-enforcement agents in this country live outside the ambit of the law. Not only snatching money here and there for rendering no services, recruitment into the army or police depends on which important army or police officer's letter of recommendation one tenders, failing which one hands in one's personal letter when "other letters" are requested, and such other letters need not be anything other than a sizable wad of naira enclosed in a full-scarp envelope addressed to nobody particularly. You better write a treatise on the moral malady of this country and circulate it wide. What is happening in this state is true of other states, variations being a matter of degree. Believe it or not you and your handful of angels are the odd men out."

"I am happy you admit there is a handful of fairly good people. Those of you who refuse to see evil in doing the wrong thing are dazzled by the glare of gold. If you were told twenty years ago you would be an apostle of corruption, I am sure you would have cursed the person who said it. Here you are now defending a practice you know is morally wrong, your only reason being acquisition of wealth, catching up with rich men whose scruples have been deadened by cupidity."

"Try and see my point of view doctor. I am not saying that wrong is right. What I mean is this. "If our accusers will admit that what the council has done is not atrocious by the moral standards of our compatriots, I would personally accept the crucifix and die a scapegoat for the sins of millions in this country. If our mortal sin is that the village folk are on the receiving end, the detraction is tolerable provided our tormentors will stem the tide of oppression of the poor that has plagued this country."

"You are simply begging the question, being aware that what you are asking for is an impossible ideal. Even in the civilized countries where you and I lived some time past, you cannot find a hundred percent of the population honest. We are agitated here because corruption has become so commonplace as to have tacit approval from the majority of the population. You seem to find shelter in the vulgar slogan; 'if you can't beat them, join them'. Let me state it categorically; one evil begets another. If we regard bribery and corruption as innocuous just because it enhances material wealth, sooner or later we shall find justification for other criminal acts. Then everybody will be adversely affected by one crime or another, and checking the perversion will be impossible because of wide-spread practice. If it doesn't affect you, it will affect your relations or offspring. The sooner we start rooting out evil, the better, and the most effective remedy is to start in your small world to practice moral rectitude even if it entails inconvenience for your person."

"Doc, you speak as if I have overnight turned the devil's advocate. I disown that insinuation. The fact is that you and I have found ourselves in a nasty situation we cannot change. What we need is adaptation and not a futile endeavour to cause a radical change."

"This is poor logic, chairman. If there is no evidence that we have tried and failed, what is the basis for the blanket conclusion that we can't change the situation? Your office provides a good starting point. Change your attitude to contracts, for instance, and you will see wonderful response from both councilors and contractors. Acquisition of money is not a true index of success. People who know the background of your wealth will always pout their lips in disapproval wherever you display it or throw your influence about, but if your name is an asset to you, you will continue to win people's admiration and esteem until death, poor or rich. I am not preaching to win you over but it is a universal fact."

"Dr Ume, I think we have laboured enough. The gulf between us is narrowing down. We can thrash out the remaining differences over refreshment. What would you have for dinner?"

The doctor glanced at the wall clock behind him and found it was past eleven. "My goodness! I will have nothing. My meal time is long past. I better starve than have any solid food now. It will constipate me. Please give me a bottle in one continuous draught, he dashed out and zoomed away, feeling disappointed at the vicious mental metamorphosis his friend had undergone."

CHAPTER VII

Education Secretaries summoned the head teacher's meeting as promptly as the message was urgent and addressed them with equal fervour to match their exhortation and underline the urgency. A good number of the Secretaries had little of their own message to add while a few others ingeniously grafted their own directives. In Ikpem Local Government Area, the secretary had estranged himself from many teachers with discriminatory promotions and transfers of head teachers. Recovering the lost honour by ingratiation appeared more remote to him than through intimidation and blackmail. Anticipating an unwholesome response, he adopted the tactic of George Orwell's Squealer by literally frisking from his table to the rear of the assembly and back to the middle in a split second, giving the impression that he wanted to be more audible.

"Ladies and gentlemen, the last part of my message touches on a very important aspect of school work which has recently been abused by teachers and head teachers alike. The abuse has caused strained relationships between head teachers and some members of their staff. My office has been flooded with reports of head teachers misappropriating hand-work (crafts) proceeds. I bet you, copies of some of these reports are on the commissioner's table at the state headquarters. I want to use this opportunity to streamline hand-work activities in the school system in this local government. Hand-work is included in the school curriculum to nurture pupil's manual skills to creativity. Children of below average intelligence and those from poor homes who may not go beyond the primary school can fend for themselves as adults through the right application of their manual talents. This aim is brutally defeated when pupils are made to contribute money – no matter how small – instead of artefact."

As he pronounced the last word, some low whisper filtered into his ears. Looking fixedly at the direction, he asked, "what is the matter over there?"

A tremulous voice replied: "I wanted my neighbour to explain to me what you mean by artefact."

"Shame! A head teacher of your experience doesn't know what is meant by artefact. Why didn't you ask me directly? It means hand-work products. The point I was making before the interruption was that pupils should be taught crafts making, and whatever they produce should be praised and accepted. No child should give money in lieu of products. Hand-work period is not another time for games when teachers engage in gossips, leaving the pupils to their fate. It is a period when teachers teach pupils handicraft or supervise them do their own craft. Every fortnight or preferably month, pupils surrender their finished products to the school. The teacher in charge will sell them and render accounts to the school treasurer who keeps the money until there is need for the proceeds. At the end of each term, hand-work returns are made to my office, showing income and how expenditure was incurred."

There was a volcano of unified protest. It took the chairman of head teachers conference almost a quarter of an hour to check the eruption. Nevertheless the secretary had no intention of yielding ground until he had articulated his jeremiad in full. When the chattering died down, he continued: "It is unethical, unprofessional and avaricious of a head teacher to use hand-work money as his or her own bona fide income. Neither does it sound decorous for a head teacher to organize a staff party at the end of the term or school year with hand-work proceeds. The Ministry does not supply attendance registers and diaries free of charge; exercise books for teachers' lesson notes must be provided by the school, likewise chalk and other teaching aid. The so-called special hand-work, if it must be collected, will require clearance from my office. I must be satisfied that the project for which it is meant is permissible. All these directives must be complied with forthwith, and any breach will be drastically dealt with."

He beheaded the surging storm of protest by asking for questions.

"Sir", that was a female voice, "you stipulated approved items of expenditure which demand dipping into hand-work money without mentioning transport claims; at the same time your office no longer gives running cost to schools but requires returns from us. Are head teachers supposed to run their schools with their little salaries?"

"You see", he answered, "hand-work money will eventually be utilized by the head teacher. You will keep an accurate record of your official movement and make claims according to approved rates from hand-work proceeds."

Another question: "Sir, you seem to have forgotten games. Games equipment are very costly nowadays. Since you have virtually banned special hand-work, how do you expect us to raise money for things like footballs which cost upwards of six hundred naira, jersey, replacement of goal posts and other school property such as clocks and signboards?"

"To begin with, you are not supposed to buy very superior and expensive footballs, neither is it prudent to embark on the luxury of acquiring jerseys. Nevertheless if the equipment is vital and the school cannot afford it, a strong appeal could be made to Parents Teachers Association" (P.T.A).

"Sir, is it against education ordinance to organize a staff party if a head teacher feels that the staff have worked so hard that they deserve some from of appreciation?"

"If you feel like giving your staff a treat, you can fund it from your pocket" otherwise the staff should make monthly contributions to a sort of welfare fund from which such parties can be funded."

As uncontrollable noise which made the room vibrate cropped up once more, the secretary slipped off in the midst of the confusion and the meeting came to an unceremonious end. As the teachers dispersed, more enraged by the high-handedness of the administration than disappointed at the outcome of the meeting, comments came from everyone.

"What does this young man think we are?" asked one elderly teacher who might have taught the secretary in the primary school. "Perhaps he believes we are timid children who will be easily cowed down by high-sounding threats". "It is their usual tactic", threw in another one, "everyone in authority in this country. The admonitory speeches are capable of melting hearts of stone but approach them through their agents and you find them morally and physically weaker than criminals. In fact every highly placed public servant in this state particularly is an embezzler in one way or another. You see how sternly he warned us against embezzlement of hand-work money. Does the local, state or federal government provide any fund known as hand-work money? How can one embezzle money which belongs to one? Hand-work money, in my opinion, is the pupils' little contribution to the running of the school. It belongs to the head teacher as much as the school itself does. He wants to divert attention from the real embezzlement which is going on in his office. The federal government certainly makes provision for running costs and equipment yet we are kept in the dark about these funds, and no school gets a piece of chalk free of charge."

"The secretary is, pure and simple, a politician", contributes another teacher. "His language has a political over-tone. He will always protect his position with threats and blackmail. However he gets away with it because a good number of the head teachers in this local government bought their promotion to head teacher status from him.

That robs them of moral strength to voice their feelings against him. The few who are not committed to him can be easily bought over with a small amount of money. If there are any who would not mortgage their conscience to him, they will speak out at the risk of being declared persona non-grata. He kicks them like balloons from one unpopular school to another."

"Unpopular in what way?" asked one of them.

"Why do you pretend?" In this age when schools are starved of funds by the local government administration, a school with a small population is unpopular. Hand-work yields practically nothing. Some schools are far away from headquarters and so are equally unpopular."

"These facts would not bother me if I was paid my right salary", replied the questioner. "I fear, like many other teachers, that I am denied part of my salary for no just cause. Nobody dare complain but we feel cheated."

"Never mind that for we have no data or evidence to establish a case. What I want is: let the much approved for me be paid promptly so as to enable me to provide my needs as they arise. Our people have a saying that any animal which does not eat the flesh of another animal will not have fat in its body. The tendency to cheat has now been sanctioned by widespread practice in our country. Every local government administration, every ministry, every corporation top personnel has its own unique loopholes and tactics for cheating both low-income employees and the administration itself. False receipts are usually conjured up by agents while genuine ones are hundred percent inflated."

"So, we men of little consequence should swallow injustice, because it is practiced in every sphere of activity in this country."

"What can we do? Assert your right and the consequences will be insufferable for you. If your assertion threatens to expose the faults of the top-dogs, they can trump up charges against you overnight and forward their reports to the ministry before you know what is happening. Only a foolish fellow would dare risk his job in this period of stark privation."

"Your opinion", concluded the originator of the dialogue "seems backed up with hard facts or experiences of real victims. This new pretence of retiring experienced teachers in order to make room for new ones has given our local authorities another opportunity of forcing bitter pills down our throat. Mark it, recommendation for retirement will be selective, depending on how docile one is, or one's capability of meeting their financial demands. Let us seal up our lips for you never can tell who will make themselves informants on fellow teachers so as to be in the authorities' good books."

CHAPTER VIII

"I have headache of an unusual type", complained Mr Igbokwe to his wife. My eye balls seem to be coming off."

"You need a lot of rest, dear. By the way do you ever have a leave? I advise that you take a month's leave and travel away from this cumbersome environment. Here your mind is working on one project or another."

"That would help me a lot but this is the wrong time for it. The financial year is about ending. We must tidy up our accounts. Government auditors could visit us unannounced.

"You don't talk of your health first. What in the world is your accounts-head doing? What is the sub treasurer there for?"

"You don't understand. The sub treasurer will not render account of the expenditure incurred by the council. He has his own definite duties. The accounts head will be guided and directed by me."

"That will do for now. Let me not make your headache severer but take note of it, a dead man has no earthly account to render. After all who are government auditors? Are they foreign chartered accountants? Aren't they bribe-ridden civil servants whose mouths can be sealed with a couple of thousand naira? Take care of your health please."

There could be no more salutary advice than his wife's piece but Mr. Igbokwe had internal problems generating the migraine which he alone could terminate. If he went on leave, a lot of irregularities were bound to be exposed to anyone relieving him, and, who ever trusts a fellow civil servant when money is at stake? Perhaps the safe half-way house could be taking a week's casual leave with his office locked up during the week. That would give him the opportunity to get medical attention without endangering his position.

In spite of the eroded confidence he had suffered in his friend, he didn't believe that any doctor other than Dr. Ume could give the badly needed relief in the shortest possible time. He decided, in spite of his discomfort, to report at Dr. Ume's hospital the next day after trying unsuccessfully to get him on the telephone. At the ticket room, he slipped his complimentary card in the palm of the nurse in charge and insisted on her showing it to the doctor at once. Soon after seeing the patient in the consultation room, he sent for Mr. Igbokwe.

"Good morning Doc."

"Good morning chairman. I hope there is no health problem".

"I am afraid there is, my head throbs a lot and I have irregular sleep. My eyeballs seem to be coming off."

Hmm! Overstrain; overwork. I warned you early enough to have enough of rest. You must take one month's leave at once."

"Doctor, I am afraid one month is too long. I can't afford to abandon my office for one month. I am on one week's casual leave."

The doctor kept silent, examined his eyes and pulled out the thermometer from under his armpit and read it assiduously.

"Lie on the stretcher", he ordered. Pulling up his shirt, and singlet, he felt his lungs with his bare palms, then placed the stethoscope on his chest for a few seconds. He did the pressure test himself. Disengaging the pressure band, he asked him to relax in his chair.

"Your health problem is not alarming yet. I strongly suspect hepatitis, but it could be incipient hypertension.

In any case, you need constant examination. I will prescribe a few hepatitis drugs but you have to report back here after four days. Perhaps you will be able to arrange for the one-month leave within the period. You need plenty of rest."

"Thank you, doctor. I will do what I can."

"John, I am not satisfied with that reluctant acceptance. You can always arrange for your leave. The problem is lack of will power. Take it if you like; if you die, the office will continue to function. Probably you haven't felt very bad yet. When you do, nobody will pressurize you to leave office work alone".

"Thank you Doc. I will comply fully."

"Bye, say hello to madam."

As his new official car glided along the laterite road to his house, the reality of the doctor's advice, his wife's prophetic warning and the sum total of the doctor's reprimand on the cantankerous visit, placed a mortal weight on his mind, thereby shooting up his temperature. He started feeling hot, the car air-conditioner notwithstanding.

"Come off it man", he seemed to say to himself. "So long as you are alive, you can always rectify any wrong. Aren't you in charge of the LGA?"

That feeling gave him momentary relief but he relapsed almost immediately on remembering the chain of unconcluded contracts; false agreements to be framed up in order to prevent large chunks of federal allocation from lapsing into the federal government coffers; end-of-the-year party which would cover up a large deficit in the balancing of accounts; above all, promotions to be hastily made and backdated a good number of months to narrow the gap between income and expenditure. To be able to forge an acceptable balance, he needed to be in entire control of his mind but at the moment he wasn't sure whether he, his physical malady or the multitude of ideas besieging his mind was in control. For the first time since he was at the peak of local authority, it dawned on him that irrational acquisition of wealth brought more restlessness than ease. Remembering the Shakespeare he studied in his secondary school days, he began to wonder how many thousands of his cheated and marginalized subjects had little bothering their minds despite the general economic hardship, while he who had a handful of good for his household and several generations of his to enjoy, could not command half an hour of uncircumscribed pleasure. Even the very privileges he thought he enjoyed turned sour on his palate when trifles impinging on his mind mirrored to him the wisdom of living a decent, if poor, life.

The bewildering decision-taking aggravated his headache. Although he regularly took the prescribed drugs, his temperature was on a steady rise. There was strong persuasion from his wife to report back to the doctor after only two days but he knew where his problem hinged.

"It is too early to go back to the doctor". He protested.

"The medicines I am taking have hardly started to act. Impatience with regard to medication results in taking an over-dose with dangerous consequences. I believe that by the end of the four-day deadline there will have been significant noticeable effects."

"Well, you know how bad you feel. You are not a baby."

The next day, his accounts head was at his house presenting vouchers and cheques to be signed. "Sir you left no directive" about the agricultural exhibition coming on next Friday. I know you wouldn't resume duty by that date. There is transport to arrange for the traditional dancing group, prizes to be bought and other necessary arrangements requiring money."

"Oh, I forgot all that. I will call at the office tomorrow for a few hours to…"

"You will go nowhere," snapped his wife. "If your attention is indispensable for the success of the exhibition, you better cancel it for now. It could be re-scheduled when you recover fully, otherwise authorize the secretary to take charge of the whole affair. Your absence wouldn't do any harm to the exhibition."

"Please tell the secretary to see me first thing tomorrow morning. What are these cheques for?"

"Sir, you have approved payment for the toilet rolls and beverages supplied by Madam Jimo. She called yesterday for her cheques. I advised her to call again tomorrow."

"Do we owe her so much?" Remember that his ten percent kick-back was part of the approved amount, he looked at the accounts head blankly, then bent down and signed the documents. Before handing him the cheques he said, "Tell her to see me at the office a fortnight from tomorrow. Don't bring me any more cheques for signing no matter the urgency. If I improve, I will report at the office some time next week."

"What about the exhibition arrangements, Sir?"

"Didn't I instruct you to let the secretary see me tomorrow?"

"That damned exhibition, what use would it be?" he thought "Have we not had one every year in the last two years and what improvement has it made in food production? Rather than reduce the prices of stuffs, there has been a steady escalation. The only incentive peasant farmers were enjoying has been placed far beyond their reach. Not only has the subsidy on fertilizer been withdrawn, the approved selling price to the public has been increased a thousand per cent. Worst still, we sell it here at the approved price, people buy it here and resell it in the villages at cut-throat prices."

Sound rationalization but the exhibition must go ahead. The state governor wanted it done soon in preparation for the state exhibition. For the chairman it was a matter of do or die. It was either going back to office next week with the attendant health risk or postponing it with the possible consequence of getting a query from the governor. Mandating the secretary to take charge of the whole affair was ruled out. Nothing could be more risky than getting him into the mainstream of the financial involvement of the council.

At lunch time, his wife had an awful lot of difficulty dragging him to table. He hardly took a mouthful of his favourite dish made special appetizing with seasonings. Janet needed no convincing that his health problem had taken a dangerous turn. "Go back to bed and rest", she persuaded. Late that evening, he could hardly get up from bed. His right limbs seemed paralysed and stiff. His power of speech was badly impaired. It took the combined might of the driver, Janet and the house-help to lift him from bed. With his free foot on the floor, he was half-dragged, half-lifted into the back seat of his car. Janet sat beside him and the driver sped-off. At the reception, Janet dashed out and bumped into the doctor's consultation room, thrown into agitation by the frantic ingress, ran to her aid. "What is the matter, madam?"

"I want to see Dr. Ume."

"What help can I render you at once?"

"Please send for Dr. Ume if he is around. I brought his patient to him".

"Where is the patient? Can't he come in?"

"I am afraid he can't. He needs to be helped in." The doctor was taken to the car. He ordered a stretcher and within a few seconds, he was laid on a bed. He watched his heartbeat and other vital signs.

"Nurse Philo, run to Dr. Ume's bungalow and tell him there is an emergency admission requiring his attention."

Janet added. "Tell him Mr. Igbokwe is very bad."

"Who tells you he is very bad?" asked the doctor, a little exasperated.

"Doctor, I don't need to be told that. He's been sick for almost one week. He never was so immobilized, so speechless and so inattentive to my presence."

Dr. Ume came in a few minutes later apparently unruffled.

"Thank you Doctor Uwakwe. Is there any private room not taken up?"

"Yes sir, room six is available", whispered one of the nurses."

"Take him to that room at once. I want only Dr. Uwakwe, Madam Janet and Nurse Philo in that room. He can't stand suffocation."

In the room, he turned to Janet and asked: when did this development take place?"

"He was almost normal until lunch time. He had no appetite. I tried in vain to make him take a morsel of food. I then let him go to bed. When I went to give him his evening drug, I found he could scarcely move his limbs. He spoke in whispers, finding it more difficult to gesticulate than whisper."

"All right, you can leave him now. He is weak but not in a dangerous state. One of my suspicions is about to be proved real."

Reluctantly Madam Janet left the room after lots of reassurances that her husband's condition was not hopeless.

"His temperature is very high. When it comes to normal, he will respond better. Nurse, strip him to his pants and massage him thoroughly with cold water; then place a working fan beside his bed. Administer these injections at once. I will return to see him in two hours' time. Dr. Uwakwe is around in case he needs attention.

At the reception he addressed Madam Janet". You can go home now. He is in safe hands. Go and see to the needs of the kids you left alone. I wouldn't want you back here until tomorrow morning."

"No doctor, I will sleep in that room where he is."

"No! Not necessary. I have enough nurses who will render him better help. Besides, there is no spare bed there."

"I can sleep on the sofa in the room."

"No, I wouldn't have another patient in that room."

A week after his admission, he woke up in mid-afternoon encountering an anxious gaze from his wife. He tried to force a smile, just to reassure her but the effort failed. He signaled to a nurse who helped him to relax on the back rest attached to the head rail of his bed. A second attempt at smiling had a measure of success.

"When did you bring me here, Janet, he managed to ask. Has the exhibition taken place?"

"No questioning", interposed the nurse. "Madam, don't answer his questions."

Turning to the patient, he said, "Dr. Ume would be annoyed to learn that you conversed with anybody, much more asking questions. Madam, I hope you are happy now. He has very much improved. He needs plenty of rest and no news. You can see we never wake him up. If he goes back to sleep immediately, the better for him and us". In the evening, Dr. Ume visited. Both doctor and patient were in a very relaxed mood.

"John, you are responding very well to treatment. I would love to have you enrolled in our tennis club as soon as you recover."

"I have had the longing to enroll but office engagement precluded that".

"Yes, take this warning. So long as you are here, the office and its encumbrances must be shut off from your mind. We do not talk shops here; we discuss health and leisure, two priceless gifts from God which very few allow themselves to enjoy, but when nature registers a protest on their behalf, we spend a fortune to appease the protesting mother."

As they were conversing, a nurse placed a tray bearing a cup of tea and a bottle of malt drink on his table.

"That's for you, John. Take whichever you like."

"Thank you Doc. I would have preferred Coffee but since it isn't available, let me take malt."

"That's all right. I don't think coffee will do you good now. That doesn't mean that you will abstain from it completely but you will forget it until your nerves resume normalcy."

"I am very grateful, Doc."

Two days later, he began to complain of boredom in the hospital. The nurse he complained to fetched Dr Ume at once.

"Good afternoon, John. How are you now?"

"Very much relieved, thank you."

"I understand you feel bored. That is natural after almost two weeks of confinement. I hope you do stroll around the hospital."

"Not often except on one or two occasions I saw my wife off to the hospital gate."

"How did you feel when you came back?"

"As if I had done twenty kilometers of walking."

"There you are. You are very much improved but not quite recovered yet."

"You are quite right doctor, I would like to be discharged tomorrow so that I will be coming for check-up as regularly as you direct. I am already sick of medicines, their odour makes me feel like vomiting."

"That is exactly what it should be like. My fear is that in your house you will be exposed to the wrong visitors who will feed you with news of your local government council, the least of your requirements now. I know our people's mentality. They will feel shunned and disregarded if they are kept out so much. In any case, you will patiently complete two weeks of intensive care here before leaving. If you return for a check-up after another week, it wouldn't be bad. Please John, your life is worth much more than anything else."

Whether Mr. Igbokwe's request for discharge was motivated by genuine longing for change of environment or thirst for news from the local government council was anybody's guess, but Dr Ume was not prepared to take chances. He insisted on his remaining in hospital in spite of his expressed nostalgia, and had his way. When Janet visited that evening, she mildly reprimanded her husband for ever suggesting being discharged.

"You can't decide when you will go. The doctor knows better".

"I cherish my health more than you think but I am terribly bored here".

"What bores you? Your menu is excellent. The doctor brings you newspapers everyday. Whatever you order from home I bring it promptly. What else deserves your attention outside here"?

"I want to be a free man once more."

"You rather long to go back to prison. Patiently gather enough energy before returning to your hell of office."

"Who mentioned office now? I want to see my house once more."

"Childishly funny, aren't you? How many months have you been away from your house?"

The conversation was interrupted by the rattling of containers on a trolley pushed by a nurse dispensing evening doses.

"This is one of my headaches now, I have a strong phobia for medicines. Even when I drink water, the very cup I use has a distasteful odour of medicine on it, even if the cup is fetched fresh from the store."

"Dear, you will soon get over it. How many days have you left?"

The remaining four days wore off dreadfully slowly. His nostalgia and medicine phobia were compounded by impatience so much that Dr Ume made him spend the last night in his house. The following morning, they drove the short distance to the hospital together. Back in his private ward, the doctor addressed him before his wife and the driver arrived.

"You are quite healthy now; your appetite and temperature are normal. I wouldn't bother you with more drugs. The only medicine I prescribe is rest. At home walk round your yard morning and evening. In the hot sun, retire to your bed and see no visitor then no matter the insistence. You will live to do your office work if you will religiously avoid that office for another week. I will expect to see you here a week from today. You may resume duty the following day".

"Doctor, I am at a loss what to say. I don't know how to express my gratitude."

"You have nothing to bother about. Just thank God that you were brought here before too late."

The check-up was a mere formality.

"You are hail and hearty, John. You have to return to the office gradually. By this I mean that you do minimal work for the first two days; then increase the period gradually to avoid sudden tension likely to occur in convalescence period. I will make time to see you within a fortnight."

Mr. Igbokwe was all gratitude. He had a good word for every nurse and doctor around. Just as he was sitting on the sofa in his ward, his driver pulled up at the hospital gate. Janet walked gracefully into his ward and warmly embraced him. She outdid her husband in expressing gratitude. She was more exuberant in her chat with the nurses who gave her mirthful congratulations on the recovery of her husband.

As the doctor had metaphorically remarked earlier, nature had protested on behalf of leisure against the chairman. As he got less and less involved in financial intricacies in the council, his health became more vibrant and he learnt the lesson of sufficient relaxation.

Dr. Ume paid him the promised visit. The entertainment was lavish to the distaste of the doctor. No amount of gratitude could equal the special attention given to him. To add to it, he paid for only drugs.

"I haven't come to receive equal compensation for the treatment I gave you. As an old-time friend, I owe you that kind of priority attention, our differing views on many aspects of life notwithstanding."

Before he left, he reminded Mr. Igbokwe of the Club he mentioned to him when he was in hospital, believing strongly that membership of it would offer him the much-needed diversion from office engagement. "I don't mean that you should join immediately. You needn't engage in anything strenuous within your convalescence period. If you approve of it, I expect you to enroll in the next three months."

"That is a safe margin. I shall have taken a decision by that time. Now you have more time to yourself, I would very much appreciate regular visits".

"Thank you very much. Perhaps the club thing might remove the necessity for that since we shall see each other almost every evening."

"Well, but Janet would like to see you more often than before."

"I wouldn't rule out occasional visits in the company of my wife."

"That's a good idea Doc. Bye and say hello to Madam."

CHAPTER IX

In obedience to the commissioner's injunction, local government education secretaries went on routine inspection tour of the schools within their jurisdiction. Their experiences were a mélange of commendable and frustrating attempts at imparting knowledge or ignorance. The serious minded ones among them spent more time teaching than watching lessons. On one of such visits, Mr. Ejeme, the education secretary of Ikpem Local Government Area, ran into a serious dilemma. Having been a party to the unorganized conspiracy to post favourite female teachers at points of easy contact, he was always more inclined to visit the schools where his clients were posted. He arrived at the particular school when the teacher in question was teaching a lesson on English language. The topic was simple past tense and the class was elementary three, a class generally believed by head teachers as being most suitable for inexperienced teachers in the sense that it was assumed a good foundation must have been laid in the first two years of primary school studies. The enthusiastic teacher remembered well that she was taught in method class that English lessons are best taught in sentences.

Before the secretary entered her class, she was drilling her pupils in oral sentences. Now she wanted to impress her admirer that her teacher-training lessons were still in her subconscious. She wrote three of her sentences on the black board:

My mother cooked yam yesterday,

What did your mother cooked yesterday?

What did she cooked this morning?

"Chima, answer the first question."

"My mother cooked ricr yesterday."

"Good. James, answer the second one."

"My mother cooked beans this morning."

"Excellent. Ibe, ask Mary what her mother cooked yesterday."

"Mary, what did your mother cooked yesterday?"

"She cooked yam."

"Very good, you have answered the questions very well."

The secretary would not embarrass his friend before her class. He did not draw her attention to the error. Instead he offered to test the class with his own set of questions.

"Elementary three children, I can see you are doing very well and your teacher is doing her best. Let us answer other questions: You sitting in the middle of the third row, what is the past tense of eat?

"It is ate".

"Spell it". A-t-e.

"Class, clap for him."

"You sitting right at the back, what did you eat this morning?"

"I eat garri this morning."

"We have been taught that the past tense of eat is ate. Could you repeat your sentence, putting <u>ate</u> in place of <u>eat.</u>

"I ate garri this morning."

"Good. Now Mary, ask the girl sitting on your right what she ate yesterday."

"Veronica, what did you ate yesterday?"

"No, that is wrong. You can't say "<u>did ate.</u>"

"But our teacher told us not to mix up present tense with the past tense".

"That is right. We are not mixing them up. <u>Did</u> helps <u>eat</u> to do its function. When we see <u>did</u> in a sentence, the verb it is helping cannot be in the past tense. The sentence is already in the past tense. Examples are as follows:

John <u>did</u> not <u>sleep</u> last night

Ibe <u>did</u> not <u>write</u> a letter yesterday

<u>Did</u> your father <u>go</u> to Aba yesterday?

<u>Did</u> your mother <u>do</u> her work today?

What <u>did</u> your teacher <u>say</u> this morning?

"Teacher, please drill them on this pattern of the past tense. Don't let

them fall back to their old error."

"Thank you sir, good bye." She tapped her table and the good-bye was echoed by the classes.

Before the disappointing visit, the class had been so drilled in the 'right' sequence of tenses that both teacher and pupils found it difficult to change. "How can I reconcile what I have taught for so long with what I cannot justify or prove right?" She thought. When a few days later, her secretary friend called outside duty time, she did not hesitate to unburden her mind: "I didn't understood what you asked me to teach the children."

"Shame, Vero! How can you say I did not understood?"

"I am not a university graduate or National Certificate of Education (N.C.E.) holder. Teach me now. I can't see anything wrong in the sentence. I have obeyed the rule of sequence of tenses."

"I am afraid you haven't. You have seriously infringed grammar. I didn't want to use the term auxiliary for your pupils, it might be a little strange to them. Some verbs are called auxiliary or helping verbs, for instance, <u>shall</u> go, <u>will</u> come, <u>does</u> like, <u>can</u> do. "In each pair, the first word is called an auxiliary verb because it helps the main verb to express itself. English grammar rule says: in changing the tense of such verbs to the past, you simply change the tense of the auxiliary verbs, thus: <u>should</u> go, <u>would</u> come, <u>did</u> like, <u>could</u> do. So you should say, I did not understand the lesson you advised me to teach my pupils. Try and understand it so that you do not continue to give your pupils wrong information. If the wrong lesson sticks now they are very young, it will be impossible to get out of the error."

"Thank you sir, we weren't so well taught in secondary school".

"You must have been but you probably have forgotten because you have been divorced from your books for so long. How long ago did you open a book before your recruitment"?

"Never mind that sir, I had no examination in view. Sorry, I am a bad host. I never offered you kola, instead I bother you with my classroom problem."

"That's more important than the kola. Primary education is child-centered. Everything possible must be done to ensure that the children get the right stuff from the word go, otherwise we are building on sand."

While her visitor sat on the only chair in her one room apartment, she moved round the chair uneasily and aimlessly, then slumped onto her bed and gesticulated, adding orally, "come closer; I have something confidential to whisper to you."

Mr Ejeme sat on the bed beside her, believing that he was being invited more for fondling than anything more serious than that.

"Yes, what was it you wanted to impart to me"?

"When are you leaving?"

"Is that the important information you wanted from me or to give me?"

"No, that isn't it but tell me frankly when you intend to leave."

"I will leave when I feel like. Do you expect more visitors?"

"Not at all. I was going to complain that I don't have much company here. I wish you would visit daily."

"That would expose me to suspicion from my wife. If I leave our house once in a while, she will regard my absence as being necessitated by extension of my office duty. She will certainly frown at my overdoing it."

"That is a good idea and a more reason why I should have you as long as possible when you come."

"Well, I am not leaving yet. What can you offer me"?

"You know how much you pay me. What can I boast of other than myself?"

"That's generous enough. You are more than a boon."

As they enjoyed caressing and pleasantries, she whispered; "You have not bought me the gown you promised me last month."

"I haven't forgotten it. I will buy it when next I go to town."

The leave-taking was difficult but eventually accomplished after Vero had hung on the secretary's car door for almost one hour discussing nothing practically serious.

Vero's bungling with English grammar was not a singular occurrence. On another occasion and at another school, an experienced teacher of not less than six years standing was teaching Mathematics in Elementary four. After adding up a number of fractions, he arrived at a sum of $\frac{14}{24}$ and left it in improper fraction form.

"Children, do your corrections following this pattern..." Mr Ejeme could not overlook such crass ignorance. "Wait a minute, children. Teacher, that is an improper fraction. Reduce it to a proper fraction."

"I can't understand sir. Isn't that a real fraction?"

"It is but needs to be reduced to lower terms."

"I still don't understand you, sir."

"Can't you find a number which can divide both numerator and denominator evenly?"

"I don't know, sir."

"Give me a piece of chalk. Class, can two divide 14 without remainder?"

"Yes sir."

"So 2 dividing 14 gives what?"

"Seven sir."

"Can 2 divide 24 without a remainder?"

"Yes sir."

"Now, divide 24 by 2. What is the answer?"

"Twelve."

"Now place 7 over 12 thus $\frac{7}{12}$, and that is the answer. You must always reduce your fraction until it is no longer possible for any number to divide both numerator and denominator without a remainder. Take note that you must divide the two components with the same number otherwise you get the wrong answer."

Without bothering to save the teacher embarrassment he added. "Teacher, I hope you equally understand it."

"Yes sir, thank you."

"Did you write notes on this lesson?"

"Yes sir,"

"Let me see it."

The teacher handed the note to him. He saw the very error in the lesson notes; then went straight to the head teacher.

"Did you read this lesson note, Head teacher?"

"Sure, I do mark my teachers' notes."

"Why didn't you discover this error?" and be showed the wrong section of the note to him.

"Sorry, I don't read experienced teacher' notes meticulously. I assume they know what to do but I carefully mark newly recruited teachers' notes. I know they need to be prodded."

"What a culpable assumption! What guarantee have you that the so-called experienced teachers' notes are error-proof? You have to read and correct every note before appending your signature. Return this note to Mr Ebere later. I do not need to be here always. I have many other schools to visit besides my office work. One of the reasons for making a head teacher class-free is to enable him or her to occasionally watch teachers at work and offer help where necessary. You don't have to sit in your office always. You are supposed to be the most experienced teacher on the staff."

The head teacher avenged himself on the staff at a subsequent staff meeting. "You subjected me to humiliation and embarrassment the day our education secretary visited us. It is shocking that a grade II teacher does not know the difference between proper and improper fractions. That is a primary school lesson. I cannot go through that humiliation a second time. I have been wrong in assuming that the experienced ones among us know what to do and write good notes. I will henceforth scrutinize your notes and make necessary comments. I shall require your notes on Friday after school so that I go through them during the week-end. In addition, we must be prepared to take corrections in good faith. To save yourselves embarrassment, take me into confidence any time you find a topic too difficult to teach. I will teach it as a sort of demonstration lesson during the appropriate period for it. The class will be informed beforehand that the head teacher will teach them a lesson at the specified time. If you do not require such help prepare your lesson very well before presenting it to your class, otherwise, I will relieve you of it if you start making a mess of it."

The worst incident resulting from teachers parading ignorance was an altercation between a teacher and a pupil from a literate environment. It was a reading class and the teacher took up a passage on bakery. After reading the first few sentences, she turned to Okey, about the best reader in the class.

"Okey, take it from me and read the next two paragraphs."

Okey rattled the whole thing perfectly.

"Your reading was excellent but you mispronounced the word flour. It is called floor."

"No Miss. Mummy says it is pronounced like "flower". Last week Sunday, as she was preparing dough nuts, I found a weevil in the flour she poured on the bowl. I told her weevils had attacked the "floor" and she insisted I should call it 'flower.'"

"What is your mother?"

"She is a banker."

"No."

"She is wrong. Please call it 'floor.'"

"Miss, I took it to Daddy, a university student who confirmed it is pronounced like flower."

"You believe your parents are right and I am wrong. Then you must go to them to teach you. I am too ignorant to teach you."

"Miss, I didn't say that. We disagreed only on pronunciation".

"Class, you remember some day last week, the very Okey rejected my pronunciation of leopard."

"Yes, we do, Miss."

"James, take him to the head teacher and tell him I can't have Okey in my class until he recognizes me as his teacher."

"Yes Miss."

"Kneel down, you naughty boy," the head teacher bellowed. "What did you say to your teacher?"

"Please sir, I didn't insult or disobey her. I told her that flour should be called 'flower' instead of 'floor'."

"Tell me the truth. Is that all you said?"

"Yes sir. I told her my parents taught me the right pronunciation."

"If it turns out that you were rude to her, I will punish you severally".

"Yes sir."

"Sit on that bench until I see your teacher."

During break time, the pupil was sent out of the head teacher's office while his teacher was brought in.

"Miss Nonye, what was the matter with Okechukwu?"

"The boy is fond of challenging me. Last week he told me before my class that leopard should be called 'Lepard.' Today again he insisted on saying 'flower' instead of 'floor,' always presenting his parents' teaching as reliable. Then I told him I am too ignorant to teach him. He should go to his parents to teach him."

"Was he rude to you in any way?"

"Isn't that challenge rude enough? Does he have to call me ignorant to become rude?"

"Take it easy, teacher. I do not see anything bad the boy said".

"Then I am going away and will not teach him any longer", and she turned to leave the office.

"Stay where you are, insolent girl! Your upbringing is "excellent." If you can treat your immediate head so shabbily barely six months in the job, you will slap those who will work with you when you have taught for three years. You new recruits have no job pride to keep up yet. Having stayed so long away from a learning and teaching environment, it is just fair to refer to you as reverting to illiteracy. Why didn't you approach me when the boy disagreed with you? You have to be very tactful in handling children whose parents are literate. In some private schools, you have pupils who speak far better English than their teachers. Those teachers learn from them instead of taking offence. In the two cases you mentioned, the boy is right and you are wrong. Re-admit him into your class at once."

The teacher left the office shedding tears. The next day, she was at the education secretary's office, asking for a transfer.

"You don't request a transfer orally. It isn't a personal affair between us. You have to put it in writing. In any case, you can't ask for transfer yet. You will be at your school for a minimum of three years before we consider transferring you to another school. However, your head teacher reserves the right to request that you be sent to another school if you prove to be too stubborn for him".

"Sir, I cannot stand his harsh language. He seems to respect the parents of our pupils more than he has regard for us."

"Tell me frankly what happened between you and him. Did he request sex from you?"

"Gush! He dare not. He could be my father."

"You must have reasons for disliking him."

"Yes, he encourages pupils to be rude to their teachers."

"No other teacher on your staff has complained of it. Are you the only teacher affected, possibly because you are the least experienced?"

"I don't know. Please think seriously about my request."

"Sending you on transfer so soon would be a bad precedent. I will see your head teacher some time next week and talk it over with him".

"That wouldn't help me. He is a big man like you. He will easily convince you that I am wrong."

"He is not a big man like me. I am his boss. He is my employee like you."

"But he behaves as if he is next to the local government chairman."

"Go back to your school. I will see you later."

Most of the reports taken to the education secretary by the fresh teachers were frivolous. They depicted their difficulty in adjusting to disciplined life after living almost uncontrolled for several years after their training. He dismissed them as such but went out of his way to treat one of them in an unethical manner. One of his mistresses returned to school late on a Monday afternoon after an over-stretched weekend. She wanted to sign the time book but the head teacher tucked it away in his drawer.

"Where is the time book?" she asked in a tone more arrogant than apologetic.

"What do you want the time book for at a quarter to 1 o'clock? Go home and regard yourself as being absent without permission today."

"Sir, let me sign the time book. I am in school today."

"What are you going to do now? In the next fifteen minutes your pupils will disperse."

"Keep it where you like. At worst you report me to the commissioner for education and he will have my job. I am used to joblessness."

She left the school and went straight to thes's office, hoping to forestall what she expected the head teacher to do.

"Good afternoon, sir."

"Miss Nwike, why did you leave school before dismissal? You couldn't have arrived here now if you left after one o'clock."

"It is that bully of a head teacher who makes himself a little god. He wouldn't allow me to sign the time book simply because I was a few minutes late today."

"I do not believe he would do that if you were a few minutes late. He would allow you to sign below a line he drew indicating late comers."

"I don't know, whatever I do irritates him. Already he has given me a query."

"That is not a serious one. There is no copy of it here. Did you answer the query?"

"I didn't."

"Whatever be your offence, it has become more grievous because of your failure to answer the query. Giving of a query is routine action meant to call employees to order. Whenever you are given one, it doesn't mean that you have been found guilty of the alleged or suspected offence. The giver will confirm or change his impression of the matter, depending on your explanation and the manner in which you put it. Why did he give you the query?"

"He said I didn't do manual labour along with my pupils."

"That would be madness. Surely he didn't say that."

"So I have become a liar. Come to our school and ask other teachers".

"One or two teachers have brought reports against your head teacher. I may have to be there some time next week to see what is going on in that school."

"That will be a good opportunity for us to air our grievances. No teacher is happy in that school."

"Go away now and make sure you don't miss school any day without informing him before-hand, and avoid going to school late."

"Mama sends greetings. I was home over the week-end."

"I see. What did you bring from home?"

"I wouldn't bring it to your office. You have to come."

"Bye and obey your head teacher."

"Please don't fail to come next week."

At 5.30 pm. Mr Ejeme pulled up besides Miss Pati Nwike's room. The whizzing of the engine woke her up. She rushed out half-clothed.

"Lazy girl, you sleep till 5.30. Have you any engagement for tonight?"

"What about reading a novel or magazine?"

"That is sad. Since you have decided to teach, you must read always in order to be sure of the information you give your pupils."

"I hardly have any book here; only one or two back numbers of 'Ladies' magazine which have little to offer as regards fashion."

What about the books you used in school, especially at Teacher Training College (T.T.C)?"

"I have given all away to my relations and friends."

"You have to buy a few good novels, African Writers series in particular, and one popular magazine for current affairs. Perhaps you do not know; in the village, teachers are regarded as moving encyclopedias. Your pupils and even their parents will always consult you for current information on politics, education and business transaction."

"They can regard me as anything they like. My priority is house-hold property, basic ones. I remember I requested help to buy a gas cooker but you turned it down. I do not have a farm here. Where can I gather firewood from? It is an offence to send pupils into the bush to fetch firewood for their teacher. A portable gas cooker would save me a world of inconvenience. Sit down, sir. Mother prepared special dish which I hope you will enjoy."

"What must that be?"

"Vegetable soup with snail and sliced oil beans."

"If it is well prepared, it is really palatable and nutritious. Pati, your head teacher was at my office after you left."

Don't mention that nasty man to me now; you will spoil my appetite".

"I equally enjoy the meal. I will drop the topic until I visit your school but do not overstay when you go on week-ends. By the way, where did you go?"

"Home of course. Where else would I go?"

"Have you no friend anywhere to visit?"

"It is you alone and I can't visit you."

"Me a lone?" How long ago did you know me?"

"Sir, are you growing jealous already?" Please I have no other one. That explains why I have nothing in my house. My counterparts who have businessmen or civil servant friends have everything they desire."

"You will have your fill. Simply guarantee that no other man has access to you."

"Am I going to isolate myself from all other men?"

"You know what I mean. Play your cards well."

"That is exactly what I am doing."

Before Mr. Ejeme left, he gave Pati a cheque for two thousand naira to purchase a medium gas cooker.

The following day, Mr. Ojo of the customs department with whom she spent the long week-end delivered a gas cooker with its accessories. The blaring of pop music from the cassette player in his car took Pati along memory lane to the lonely road they drove for more than half an hour on the last Sunday evening she spent at Port Harcourt.

"Welcome Johny. Thank you a thousand times. I would have sacked you if you disappointed me. I need it badly now. The rains are approaching and firewood becomes more and more difficult to come by."

"It is a pleasure being able to oblige you in this little way."

"I hope you are not leaving tonight. Our highways are most unsafe at night. You may leave early enough tomorrow morning to get to your office before it is too late."

"Never mind, I will be there before 8.30 if I leave at 6.00 am".

Mr. Ejeme made an unscheduled visit to Pati's school the following week. He made straight for the head teacher's office.

"Mr. Ikpeama, I regret to remark that your teachers are not happy with you. What is the matter?"

"I didn't know about that sir. I thought I was getting on well with them although I kept a safe distance from everybody, being conscious of the fact that fraternity would expose me to ridicule or contempt."

"Contrary to what you thought, three of them, to be precise, have lodged complaints about you at my office."

"That is interesting indeed. My teachers reporting me instead of me doing that against them. Well, they have given me the green light."

"Perhaps we could sort out the differences now. That is why I am here now. I wouldn't like an ugly situation to develop. That wouldn't augur well for school discipline or effective teaching."

"You believe it is administratively right to summon me and my staff before you to sort out the so-called differences?"

"What is wrong with that?"

"What would be your reaction if you saw here when you arrived, one of my teachers and a pupil stating their cases against each other? If you so choose, I am at your command."

Mr Ikpeama sent a pupil handy to fetch his general prefect. "Robert, go and inform all teachers that I want them or the education secretary wants them in my office now."

Robert dashed out, and in less than ten minutes every teacher in the school was standing, apparently inquisitive in their look.

"Robert, tell every monitor to bring his teacher's chair here. Tell them also that if I hear any voice from their class in their teachers' absence, the class concerned will go for manual labour throughout tomorrow."

When the staff were seated, the secretary addressed them thus: "My dear teachers, the school is a sort of large family unit. No well-behaved child can be produced by a family that does not exist as a unit. In a good family, parents play their roles towards each other and towards their children. The latter in turn play their roles to their parents and these ensure peace and harmony. If through some misunderstanding, a loop-hole is created in the family, the result is always undesirable behavior from one or more members of the family. Eventually chaos sets in and every member bears or suffers the consequences. In the school, there is the head teacher, other members of staff and the pupils. The staff deserves their respect. If the staff quarrel among themselves, they teach the wrong moral lesson to their pupils. For school work to progress unhindered, the head teacher and his staff must work co-operatively and harmoniously. Recently I have seen some of you at my office complaining about one thing or another against your head teacher. I want those concerned and intending ones, if any, to air their grievances now so that we nip the discrepancy in the bud."

Mr Ikpeama suppressed his frothing anger and maintained a facade of equanimity. As the secretary flashed glances on the faces of the staff in eager expectation of one of them breaking the ice, the head teacher was busy arranging important school documents in his drawer. He kept the log book and the time book on his right hand side. The uneasy silence was broken by Miss Nwike.

"Sir, ask the head teacher what I have done wrong. He doesn't like me. Every time he threatens to report me to you…."

The secretary interrupted her speech: "But he hasn't done that yet".

"I don't know whether he has or not. He has given me a query. Let him tell you the crime I have committed."

"Head teacher, what do you say to that?"

Ask her what she has done correctly since she reported here."

"I don't like this bandying of words. Make your points succinctly so that she will be convinced of her errors."

"I will not continue this witch hunting. I gave her a query for what I thought was a serious fault. Since you encourage my staff to tell on me, on the basis of their report, give me a query for maltreating them. It is only then that I will say anything about my relationship with them."

"Mr Ikpeama, take it easy. I am only trying to put your shaken house in order."

"I would rather like it collapsed on my head than endure this slight."

"How can you claim to be doing the right thing when no member of staff is happy?"

"How can you encourage the staff to go against work etiquette? Did you ever ask for the log book or time book"?

You have already taken sides. By the way, how many have I reported to you? You better transfer complaining ones to safer hands or replace me with a more complying head teacher. I am disappointed at the twist you have given to staff etiquette and general discipline".

"I will not have that insult any more."

"I will not swallow your fumbling hook and sinker."

"Get your house in order to deserve my good opinion."

"Consult your head teacher for the right information."

CHAPTER X

Dr. Ume had made schedule upon schedule to visit Mr. Igbokwe again since the Sunday of a treat but each time some emergency or encumbrance cropped up in the nick of time requiring his attention. He had long concluded that Mr. Igbokwe had no inclination to be detached from his council intricacies, so there was hardly any point egging him on to join his tennis club. Yet there was need to call on him once in a while, if anything, to re-emphasise the necessity of giving priority attention to his health. Mr. Igbokwe, on the other hand, had been feeling guilty of ingratitude, having remained for about six months without returning Doc's post-recovery visit.

"Next Sunday, come rain or shine, I must make time to call on him."

That Sunday, he was accompanied by his wife. When they arrived, Dr Ume was having a late lunch.

"We do not back-bite you, Doc, That's why we have come at the right time." (Meeting someone while he is eating means you speak well of him).

"Right time? Did you ever have your lunch at 3.45 p.m?"

"That is one of doctors' occupational hazards."

"Dora", called the doctor, "we have august visitors."

"It were better you called us December visitors."

"We never had the pleasure of your company for quite some time. You have regained your lost weight, thanks to God."

"And to you too."

Dr. Ume dropped his cutlery a few minutes later in order to join them at the reception section of the living room.

"Enjoy your meal to the full", prompted Mr Igbokwe. "We are not in a hurry to leave. This evening is for you if you can spare it."

"I never very much enjoyed it. I wanted a little something in my stomach after a five-complicated operation. I was so hungry that I thought I wouldn't last the next hour if I didn't eat anything."

"What is the patient's ailment?"

"He was reduced to mince meat in a horrible road accident. We literally pieced limbs and flesh together. If he survives, we give special glory to God. He never recovered consciousness till I left the theatre. Dora, find something for Mr and Mrs. Igbokwe."

"We have certainly called on the wrong day. I know you will go into the ward to see him at regular intervals from now until he revives."

"No, I don't have to unless there are bad complications. I have a team of conscientious doctors and nurses. I have to congratulate myself on my impeccable choice. I never saw young men and women as devoted in this part of the world. It is wonderful."

"Because you set the pace. Every new comer will have to belong or drop out. Your rigid self-discipline is paying off."

As the conversation was going on Dora dropped a China plate containing chilled fried pieces of meat, some bottles of beer and malt on the centre table and gesticulated Janet away into the pantry."

"Where are you going, Janet? Aren't you partaking of this kola?"

"That's for you and Mr. Igbokwe", replied Dora.

The two women retired to the pantry at the time it was inaccessible to the children of the house, to discuss their own cherished topics.

"It appears these women read our minds, chairman", remarked the doctor. "Our different pursuits in life have reduced to a minimum the chances of our coming together when we desire each other's company."

"That's right. I anticipated you would remind me of joining your tennis club".

"No. you got me wrong. I have relinquished that persuasion. I know the suggestion never appealed to your taste. You have a right to choose what you like and reject what you do not like. We never think for adults."

"Not that I didn't like the idea but I can't really make time for it.

"That is sheer hypocrisy or a subterfuge. Sorry if my language is harsh. I find no way of mellowing it down."

"You are always down-right frank, I know, but I reject both charges. Since my bout of hepatitis, I have been trying to do the best I can with minimum effort. That creates its own problem. What I can accomplish in one week is spread out to one month or more. I am compelled to go to office at regular and irregular times. Often I work better when I am left alone after office hours".

"And you believe you are sparing your energy. You are simply shifting overstrain from office hours to leisure hours without realizing the danger. Well, in keeping with my professional obligation, I will stress once again that health is the most precious possession a living being has.

Any other possession is secondary. A really sick person loses appetite for everything imaginable."

"Doc, I have never for once disputed your invaluable advice about work and health preservation but you see we are sort of encaged in our chosen engagement. There is no going back unless one musters enough courage to abdicate. Even then, one will unleash a storm of suspicion and castigation against oneself. In my opinion, relief will come at the expiration of our tenure. If one vies for a second round, then he should lose everybody's pity or sympathy."

"I have achieved one thing as regards your chairmanship of the council: you have realized that you are in a sort of self-imposed circumscription. In a large measure, this is true of every profession one chooses; there must be checks and balances which impose discipline on us but the difference is that in certain engagements, the conscience as well as the body is fettered, and the victim displays on his face a semblance of happiness while internally he is grappling with a conscience riddled and distabilised by compunction. People in your job are treading on slippery ground. There are many tempting attractions apparently irresistible. Only people of strong moral fibre tread without slipping. Perhaps I sound decidedly anti-council; I am particularly concerned because of you. I want to see a resurgence of the honesty and forthrightness which we associated your name with in our secondary school days. It is very difficult to build up a good image of oneself but only one trifle of a mistake smudges the image indelibly."

Mr Igbokwe listened like a boy about to undertake an adventure characterized by risk and ultimate fortune. He admired Dr. Ume's altruistic endeavours to salvage a near – hopeless wreckage, but self pride had the better of him.

"Doc, I must be honest with you. You have always shown particular interest in my public image for which I should be grateful. Whether I share your views on general morality or not, I must cherish that gesture but I crave your tolerance. The council and all it stands for have been painted blacker than hell by some people in the society whose character and means of living are most dubious, and very few people ever bother to challenge them. On the contrary, their display of criminally acquired wealth wins general admiration. I will accept the charge of hypocrisy if it is leveled on all of us in this society. It appears we have accepted without question the theory that the end justifies the means".

"Some have definitely, not all of us."

"The exceptions are negligible."

"Negligible does not imply a hundred per cent negative. It rules out any generalization in this regard.

My advice is: You and I should belong to the negligible few for the good of posterity."

At this point Janet and Dora emerged.

"What debate has absorbed you so much?" asked Dora humorously.

"They must be re-living their past experiences", replied Janet on their behalf. "Each time they come together, it is either their secondary school days or their ordeal overseas. I wish they belonged to the same profession. Isn't it time we left, Mr Chairman?" All laughed at the humour.

"Yes, we must be going. Doc, make time to call before long. You have worked up the passion in me; you will work it down or I do it."

All right, good night rare visitors. I will return the gesture soon."

The Association of Principals of Teacher Training Colleges were to have their annual conference at Ugigi. Attendance to the conference was very good. No principal was absent or sent a deputy. One of the principals from Oji State made a grandiloquent address, ex-raying the progress of teacher training in his state and was spotlighted by a representative of the Federal Ministry of Education who cornered him at the end of the morning session.

"Mr Principal from Oji State, I listened to your report with special interest. We in the Federal Ministry of Education did not know that such a renovation was going on in Oji State. I like to have more details of it. When I get back to the capital, I shall intimate my ministry of the innovation. We shall monitor the progress of the new trend. If it works out successfully, we may pass on the idea to the other states. Meanwhile tell me as much detail as you can recall: what prompted the T.C. I course? How does it work in practice? By this I mean the course content, conditions of entry and advantages to the trainees and the school system."

"Sir, furnishing you with these details will require at leas an hour which we do not have now. We have barely twenty-five minutes between our lunch and the afternoon session. The alternative is foregoing our lunch."

"The desired information is worth it. We can chat over snacks and coke over there at the gate."

The suggestion was accepted and the enquirer offered to pay for their refreshment.

"Yes officer, your questions are multifarious. I shall do what I can to answer them satisfactorily. First of all, the state government was finding it very difficult to provide adequate teachers for Junior Secondary School (JSS) pupils as a result of lack of the right caliber of middle-class teachers to handle important subjects necessary for the

154

implementation of the 6-3-3-4 scheme of education being implemented in the country. Subjects like Introductory Technology, Integrated Science, Agricultural Science, Physical and Health Education, Music etc., suffered mishandling and, in extreme cases, abandonment. The State Schools Management Board (SSMB) has always complained of high salary bill for teachers. It was therefore, unimaginable for the state government to recruit more qualified teachers. The SSMB had to fall back on what it had. It was thought reasonable and economical to pick some primary school teachers for retraining in order to groom them for manning the JSS course. I hope I have answered the first question – what prompted the course."

"You have indeed, but what happens to the vacuum you are creating in the primary schools from where you draw your trainees?"

"Recruitment of unemployed trained teachers was done fairly recently to offset the loss so caused."

"I can understand that. You said earlier it was unimaginable for the state government to recruit qualified teachers. It is reasonable to believe that fresh primary school teachers will cost the state government much less."

"The course is open only to serving teachers because it entails study leave with salary. We cannot pay those who have not been working for us. There is no formal entrance examination. Applicants are interviewed and successful candidates are selected. The lists are sent to the various colleges where they will be trained. To start with, only a few subjects are covered: Mathematics, Introductory Technology – a new subject in the state, Integrated Science, Agricultural Science, Physical and Health Education, Music and the Vernacular. The English language is compulsory for all students, also principles and practice of education. These subjects are taught at different colleges and the course lasts for one year. The students are subjected to serious examination at the end of their course. Their answer scripts are centrally marked by Ministry of Education officials. Successful ones are awarded Teachers Grade I Certificate and that means automatic promotion to another cadre. The ministry is thus killing two birds with a stone: cheaply providing the needed middle man-power for the school system and doing selective promotion without inciting protests from any quarters. This is the T.C. I course in a nutshell."

"The scheme appears a laudable one to me. Perhaps if funds were available, it could be expanded to include primary school subjects, and organised in such a way that primary school teachers would go for the retraining in such rotation as not to disrupt school work. In my opinion, primary school teachers need some form of regular refresher courses, because the qualitative education we so much clamor for depends on the quality of teaching at the basic level."

"Sir, this is labouring the obvious. The new experiment has revealed that more than fifty percent of primary school teachers have reverted, or are at the verge of reverting, to illiteracy. This is the most sensible and pragmatic step towards attaining qualitative education for our children."

"As I said before, the attention of the Federal Ministry of Education will be drawn to it. I am not making any promises. If the powers that be receive the idea kindly, some practical encouragement will be given to your state in order to make other states emulate it. It has been a pleasure chatting with you."

"What did you say was your name?"

"Mr. Ubaka, sir."

"Thank you. If you happen to visit Lagos, call on me at the inspectorate eection of the Ministry of Education, I am Mr. Oladipo"

"Thank you, sir."

The first set of T.C. I teachers had graduated but there was no mention of converting their salaries to T.C. I scale. The second set had been caught in the web of irregular salary payment. However, they regarded themselves as fortunate since they had not been owed for longer than three weeks after month-end, whereas their serving counterparts had been owed for upwards of two months.

The state wing of the National Union of Teachers (NUT) threatened industrial action if arrears of teachers' salaries were not paid off within a fortnight. The commissioner for education summoned a meeting of the top executives of the ministry to review the critical situation.

"Ladies and gentlemen, the aim of this meeting is to sound your opinion on the Sword of Damocles hanging over the ministry. The government is hard put to it implementing the budget, and by a sad irony of priority, education is a victim. The governor remains adamant to appeals to release funds for teachers' salaries. It is as naïve as foolhardy to continue to under-rate teachers. Under the umbrella of their national union, they can move mountains. Our admirable mental baby, the T.C. I course, is about to be starved to death. What a mockery we are making of our acclaimed ingenuity. My hands are so tied that I find myself defending a policy I know is blatantly indefensible. I could throw in the towel and go back to my university but I shall have betrayed a course I believed in and extolled so much. Please I want your advice."

The permanent secretary in the ministry was the first to speak.

"Commissioner sir, we all, the so-called highly placed officials of the ministry, are in similar dilemma. We cannot walk out on the government in this hour of approaching darkness. If we have any claim to ingenuity, we have to stretch it to its tether's end in order to find a palliative to our current stalemate. How can we conjure up money to pay teacher's salaries up-to-date? We have to make use of all available resources. I remember that in the SSMB account, pupils' caution fee has a different sub-head. I am not sure it has been utilized. We can divert that. The ministry is accountable only to itself. That can pay part of the arrears of salaries. We can trump up another fundraising device and call it any plausible name. What comes to my mind immediately is an insurance scheme for pupils. Three naira per head in the primary school and five naira in secondary schools will go a long way in neutralizing our debt."

The director of education, maintaining a dour countenance, made a false attempt at brightening up. "Permanent Secretary, sir", he spoke up, "why are we moving from one illegality to another? Do we pretend not have been pestered enough by both principals and parents demanding a refund of caution fees to final year students not found guilty of damaging school property? Even if we can get away with that breach of agreement and trust, how do we justify the proposed insurance scheme? Every right-thinking person will easily conclude it is a subterfuge. How can we indemnify an accident casualty involving thousands of naira when we refuse to refund a mere twenty naira to a pupil leaving school for good? I fear we are exposing ourselves to mistrust and denigration. The very phrase, trump up, belies the intension. It is suggestive of deceit. Commissioner sir, I like to dissociate myself right away from all such disparaging, face-saving ruses."

Every other person at the meeting looked at him with dismay. Was he out of his senses? They forgot his knack for dissenting from popular views when he felt that compliance would place his integrity at stake. Either their minds were befogged by the exigencies of the season or they took too much for granted. To him, the satisfaction of having voiced his apparently unpopular views without considering anybody's whims seemed to have given his personality a dominance which reduced his cowardly comrades to lilliputian size. His face assumed more contortion and his spirit was less daunted. The commissioner took a hard look at his face without effecting a change in his defiance of protocol. The permanent secretary was at a loss how to defend his proposals. By all means some officials were disposed to side with the director but were cowed down by the commissioner's indiscernible facial expression.

The eerie silence was broken by the permanent secretary.

"Commissioner, sir, perhaps the director has more realistic ideas about how to get our ship out of the doldrums. I admire frank opinions but they must not be entirely negative in a situation like ours. More concrete, positive suggestions are very necessary now."

"I am not prepared to rack my brains over this matter. Finance is outside my portfolio. The Financial Controller is here. He could liaise with the Ministry of Finance and the Accountant General to find the remedy we want."

The commissioner suddenly rose from his seat and asked tersely: "Gentlemen, has anybody any other statement to make?" There was no reaction from any quarters.

"Then we call it a day. If there is need to re-convene this meeting, you will be informed of the date at the right time.

The director of education returned to his office and started drafting his letter of resignation:

His Excellency,

Thank you for giving me the opportunity to serve the people of this state in my capacity as the director of education, an enviable post. In the last six months I have noticed the gradual but relentless collapse on my head of the edifice I am propping up, and my incessant call for help has so far attracted no sympathy or mere attention. The quintessence of man in me is in jeopardy. I will suffer irreparable loss of name and incur the curse of even unborn generation if I continue to supervise this regrettable disintegration.

Since I have no intention whatsoever of subverting government development plans or precipitating the crumbling of the state finances as a result of unreasonable demand for attention to my department, and since I have no stamina to resist pressure from teachers and their dependants, I earnestly implore you to accept my resignation with effect from the 21st of May, 1995. I will, however be prepared to make useful contributions in other spheres of the state's economic or educational development whenever it pleases your Excellency to give me another assignment.

Thanks.

Yours faithfully,

Okams Ahaneku

He read it over two times. There was no blemish in thought or expression. The first impulse was to get it typed at once but a second thought prevailed on him. "Why not discuss this with your understanding wife first?"

After dinner, children were persuaded to go to bed. The television program was deemed unhealthy for their moral growth. Then the director tabled the topic. Incidentally his wife was a teacher. They discussed it dispassionately both from the government point of view and the teachers.

"Teachers in this state have been given the shabbiest treatment ever in the whole federation. Nobody seems to have a good word for them. As far as civil servants are concerned, teachers can feed on sand. Aren't they traditionally known as poor teachers? From the 25th of every month, civil servants start getting their salaries. Teachers will be grateful to get their own after sixty days. Yet any mention of strike action is regarded as an abomination by both parents and government officials. They always have a sentimental weapon; the future of the children of this state is at stake. It doesn't occur to any of them that no one can work effectively on an empty stomach. I subscribe to strike actions."

"We had a very dramatic meeting on this problem today. Someone suggested, in addition to appropriating caution fee, starting an insurance scheme to which pupils in the primary school will contribute three naira per head and those in the secondary school will pay five naira each. I strongly expressed objection to it and the commissioner called off the meeting. He is somebody I held in high esteem but is appears to me he has been converted to the ideas of some pig-headed deadwood in the ministry. I anticipate a crumbling of the educational structure in this state in a not too long time. I wouldn't like to play the ostrich, burying my head in sand when the simoom is approaching. I have written my letter of resignation which I will hand in if you do not object to it."

He handed the letter to his wife who studied it assiduously.

"The letter is well worded and your reasons cogent but I do not think you can afford to resign you appointment now. You are no tradesman neither do you take interest in politics. What are you going to do next?"

"I believe that when one road closes another one opens. So long as I breathe I shall always find something to do. I am not burning my certificates."

"You have risen so high in the Ministry. Wherever you go now you will begin almost at the base of the ladder. You cannot pursue idealism at the expense of the family. Please submerge your individuality in the flood of collective folly. Your resignation will not improve the situation a bit."

In a tone less humorous than stern he asked, "when did you become a philosopher?"

"Your resignation letter has made me one. No one has a monopoly of knowledge. Your philosophy is idealism; mine is realism. Please do not drown my views in the misguided notion of feminine weakness. Your volition will beget economic suicide. You must make definite plans for the survival of the family before attempting financial suicide."

"My resignation will, by no means, improve the situation but what about sharing in the general smearing of image?"

"Do not deceive yourself believing that many people in this material-chasing society care very much about image. Your image is guided with wealth irrespective of the means of acquiring it."

"I will admit, your approach is more realistic than mine, so I will tear up the letter."

A couple of weeks after the still-born meeting, sets of circular letters were run off and dispatched to heads of teachers training colleges, secondary schools and local government education units, conveying major policy decisions affecting the school system in the state: T.C. I courses were to be discontinued as from the next academic year; teachers and non-academic staff of SSMB who had put in thirty-five or more years of service would be retired with effect from the end of the academic year; pupils in both primary and secondary schools were to be insured by the SSMB and parents were to make a token contribution of three naira and five naira per primary and secondary pupil respectively to the insurance scheme. The circular on insurance added: "Token contributions must be completed before promotion examinations start. However, no pupil must be sent out of school for his parents' failure to pay the levy, but the defaulting parents must not have their wards' results until the levy is paid.

The circular letter to principals advised them to inform their staff that those ripe for retirement should formally apply to the SSMB for retirement, threatening that those who failed to apply would be dismissed without benefits on discovery. At best they would be made to forfeit part of the benefit to make good the overpayment they had enjoyed. Local government education Secretaries were directed to compile lists of teachers in their local government areas due for retirement. Within a week of the circulation of retirement information, the SSMB file room was the busiest room in the secretariat complex. The attendant received a thousand and one short notes instructing him to give file No. so and so to the bearer.

"Who are you? The attendant asked the first person who gave him the officer's note.

"I am a teacher in the state."

"Is this your file number."

"Yes, why do you ask this question?"

"You are not supposed to have access to your file".

"It is my file and not yours or anybody else's."

"Tell Oga (the boss) he should send his messenger or secretary to collect it. I will not give it to you."

Dejected and angry, he left after telling off the attendant.

"Say what you like, Oga knows I am right."

"Sir, the attendant refused to give it to me. He said you should send somebody else for it."

"He is right but my messenger took a message to the Ministry of Health and the typist cannot leave this office for any reason until he has typed all the letters on his tray. Give him this note. If he fails a second time to honour my orders, then he will be subjected to disciplinary action". The note reads: "Give him the file in spite of protocol."

The poor attendant obliged without further hesitation.

As more of such notes found their way to his table, he concluded that the co-operating officer has been sufficiently gratified by the visiting teachers. If such a highly placed officer yielded to the promptings of cupidity, it would be extremely stupid of a mere attendant of messenger status not to take full advantage of the relaxation of protocol to enhance his economic welfare. The first few of his clients got their files without any hitch. Then it was either "I am hungry. I haven't had breakfast or lunch", depending on the time the visitors called, or "I am so tired I can't look for a file now". The impatient caller soon discovered that neither fuming nor pleading would effect a change of attitude; instead a few naira, however not less than five exorcised the hunger or tiredness. As the number of callers increased his thirst for naira became keener. He changed formula. He would do make-belief searching for about five minutes and declare the file missing. "If you like, come and do the searching yourself". At which shelf would the uninitiated start, not furnished with their file coding?

"Sir, if you don't mind, bring copies of your credentials and I will open another file for you or you leave ten naira for hiring a messenger from another department to help locate your file. Perhaps it is not lost but it will take weeks for me working alone to identify it in this mess of a place."

The latter alternative was always cheaper and had easy acceptance.

The receiving officer's fee was determined by the number of years the applicant's clock was to be set back. As the shoddy deal increased in number, the fox became apprehensive of repercussions from his superior officer and resorted to a mock show of severity. "You completed a form five years ago stating the exact date you started work. It is here in your file. If you make any alteration, you will risk loss of part or whole of your gratuity". So the unlucky late applicants became the actual victims of the staff pruning measure.

File up-dating took a more dramatic turn at local government level. In Ikpem Local Government Area, the secretary appointed two favourite head teachers as con men who compiled lists of teachers who desired an extension of service. One of the agents was overdue for retirement. His commission consisted in waiving the extension fee for him. Considering himself as being at a disadvantage – "loss of face and credibility" – if the odious commission leaked to the public, he decided to compensate himself in advance by exceeding his 'employer's target by a good margin. Those who passed through him felt the pinch of extortion but would rather endure it than risk being listed for retirement at a time they had practically no savings and the prospect of their retiring on a sizeable pension was non-existent as a result of the mirage of promotion to head teacher special class with its attendant skip of two salary grade levels upwards. However, before the list of obedient teachers was sent to the state headquarters of the SSMB for retirement processing, the cat was let out of the bag. The secretary summoned the over-smart agent to his office. There was a dumb show, the agent being prepared to go to any length with him.

"Why did you exceed the amount I advised you to collect?"

"How did you know I exceeded it?"

"How much did I ask you to collect per head?"

"How much did you ask me to collect?"

"I am not prepared for this ding-dong affair. There are two options open to you: give me every kobo you collected or refund the excess to those so extorted, failing which I include your name in the list to be sent to the state headquarters."

"Is it extortion because of the excess? You cannot get away with blackmail. If you include my name, I send to the headquarters the list of people you exploited and the amounts involved. Living in a glass house, you should not throw stones."

The secretary became gagged and his pent-up emotion found expression on his face and eyes. The head teacher refused to be hoodwinked. Realizing the pungency of his offensive, he unleashed a crushing blow. "A man in your position must live an exemplary life. We know most of your clandestine practices but kept quiet for goodness sake. Now you want to tyrannise us, your confidants, you must brace yourself for confrontation from near and far."

As he said this he bolted out of the office, congratulating himself on his ability to make virtue out of vice. The secretary was touched on a very soft spot. He could not compromise his personal pride and position by showing a conciliatory attitude; he was reassured by the fact of their mutual implication and his having more money to part with in order to shield himself. Above all, he had more connections at the headquarters than the poor old head teacher who was at the mercy of every wind.

Some of the junior clerks in the secretary's office who had been nursing grudges about the secretary's pandering to base financial inclination, eavesdropped very attentively. When he left the office that afternoon, the rehearsal of the drama was a big relish and a good comic relief.

"He will now stew in his own juice", one of them spoke out. "They say everyday is for the thief but one day is for the master of the house."

A more reticent one among them asked, "what do you think will come out of it? Mr. Ajani can ill-afford to have a show-down with the secretary, neither will the secretary press the issue further. It will die a natural death. Mr. Ajani is well aware of the fact that the secretary has God-fathers at the headquarters. On the other hand, the secretary has used Mr. Ajani for secret his businesses for so long that he will never regain his reputation if he pushes the old man to the point of disclosing all he knows about him. Stop these comments now. If the secretary gets to know we are interested in his secret affairs, we will stagnate on one salary grade level for as long as he is here."

CHAPTER XI

The minister of education was on a working tour of Oji State. Although his main concern was making an on-the-spot assessment of the federal institutions in the state in terms of staffing, infrastructure, equipment and financial viability, he made provision of some little time to have a bird's eye-view of the retraining program for teachers in the state on which the officer who represented his ministry at the Teachers Training Colleges Principals Conference (TTCPC) had briefed him sufficiently. In a welcome address the state commissioner for education was to present to him, a copy of which was made available to him in advance, there was no mention of the highly praised new educational experiment. What dominated the address was a pathetic appeal for financial aid to liquidate debt owed to teachers, provide infrastructure to accommodate unprecedented population explosion in secondary schools and equip school for science to meet the requirements of the 6-3-3-4 system recently introduced into the state schools system.

"Mr. Commissioner," he asked in the host's office, "What about the T.C. I course which attracted much attention at the Teacher Training Colleges Principals Conference? It doesn't seem to be a priority in spite of the general acclaim it seemed to have enjoyed at the conference."

"Honourable minister sir, we have decided to discontinue it because it is becoming increasingly financially burdensome to run. You know the teachers being retrained are on in-service course. Paying them their monthly allowances is incongruous when we are owing their counterparts in the field three months' salaries. In addition, on completing the course, they will be converted to a higher salary grade level, thus depleting further our meager financial resources. It now appears to us a luxury we cannot afford."

"Really?" Sneered the Minister. "So the course was scraped even before it took off. How many years did the experiment last?"

"Just two years sir."

"Don't you think it was too short-sighted of the Ministry to introduce a course before its viability was ascertained?"

"Apparently it is sir, we could revive it any time the necessary funds were available."

"What about waiving the study leave aspect of it?"

"The idea of study leave makes the course attractive to teachers. Stop the salary and we shall have no students."

"Well, we were thinking of suggesting the idea to other states if we found it professionally useful and well organized. Your ministry is in a dilemma you know. How do you get the required middle man-power which you proffered as the main reason for the course?"

"We shall do strict rationalization of the existing staff in the school system. Some schools apparently overstaffed, will lose some of their teachers to very needy ones."

"I wish you all the best."

A grand send-off was arranged for the visiting minister. The dignitaries living in and around the state capital, traditional rulers and top-notch local government executives were invited to the party. Dr Ume ran into Mr Igbokwe at the party.

"Hello chairman, how is your health?"

"Very well, thank you; how is your family?"

"All is well with us, thanks a lot. Sorry I haven't been able to honour my pledge. I hope Madam is not very angry with me. I still will make it."

"I am very much obliged. I was beginning to feel a little uneasy. I could call without minding who owes a return visit. I am happy you are as bereft of time as I find myself."

"Never mind, we shall make time some day. My experience is that, for a self-employed person, time never makes itself available for courting or nurturing friendship. To do it, one has to force time to be obedient."

"Doc, I don't know whether you are a better philosopher than a medical officer. You philosophise a lot on life generally."

"Much as I wouldn't agree that my remarks are philosophical, I have to admit that I read a lot of philosophical essays at my leisure. I enjoy Plato's works very much."

"It isn't a wonder that you are inclined to moralizing. Most of Plato's ideas are swaddled in morality or ethics."

"Yes Mr. Igbokwe, that remark has exhumed the buried hatchet so to speak. Now your health has returned to normal, I hope you do not spend hours on end in office stretching your reasoning faculty to exhaustion?"

"Not very much though it is unavoidable occasionally."

"Moment of frankness indeed! Old habits, they say, die hard. I am afraid you will charge me again with passing harsh judgment on you but I am sincerely complying with my natural inclination. You seem to me to exemplify the saying that the desire to have increases by having. My brutal periodic indictment has not, in the least, staunched the current of blinding wealth mania in you."

"Doc, I suppose you don't intend to re-enact our verbal duel."

"By all means. There couldn't be a better arena. A cock-tail party has the unique advantage of permitting pairs to detach themselves from the rest of the participants in order to chat undisturbed. Our elders say that where a child points at while he cries, either of his parents must be there. I want to ensure the recovery of your moral probity."

"Doctor, leave that theme alone. Each time you bring it up my mind goes pit-a-pat in spite of my efforts to maintain a courageous stance. You will only succeed in spoiling my appetite for the delicacies being served at this party".

"I feel flattered. If my importunity can evoke such a degree of uneasiness, then there is hope of eventual success. A heart disposed to unease is half won by remorse. Let us sacrifice our appetite to our discussion. The sacrifice is worth the eventual result."

"I regard this purely as an academic exercise. I will, therefore, go back to my lone but strong defence; if I were the only victim of this lethal virus, I would have long yielded to your pressure. Who does not pursue wealth in this country today, even you? Who wouldn't in a country where wealth is health; wealth is job; wealth is education for one's children; wealth is success in an election, social stigma notwithstanding; wealth is justice; wealth is prominence in the society; ad infinitum?"

"What exactly do you mean by these assertions?"

"Thank you for giving me the opportunity to expatiate on my points. How many poor can afford the cut-throat prices of medication and the prohibitive charges in private hospitals in this country today? I know you would not suggest government hospitals as a cheaper alternative since you are a man entirely guided by a sensitive conscience. Good health is now the preserve of wealthy families. Now that our public school system is in shambles, how many families can ensure good education for their children in private schools where a term's school fees are one thousand percent of those payable in public schools? Let us regard education as a luxury; what about food? You can guess as well as I, how costly justice is in this country. The litany is endless."

"Your points are indisputable but it is those social ills that you and I are bound in conscience to combat. If you can recall the trend of our first round of debate, you will agree that we have gone back to where we started:

acquisition of wealth without moral justification. This is exactly what I condemn."

"Where on earth is wealth fairly acquired? If your dictum is clean wealth, I say without mincing words, you cannot find it anywhere. A few years ago, for instance, people could rightly say private hospitals were free from corruption. I am afraid that is not true today. A patient had an operation in a renowned eye clinic in this country, not quite three months ago. The doctor prescribed two different eye drops to be applied separately to the different eyes. The nurse on duty gave him one and advised him to apply it to both eyes. The patient suspected fowl play and so applied it to the affected eye only, starving the other one. Not long after he started using it, he felt an itch in the starved eye and went back to see the doctor. The very offending nurse intercepted him and advised him to apply the same medicine to both eyes. As he was skulking, a junior nurse secretly studied his card and advised him to insist on seeing the doctor. On insisting, the meddlesome nurse admitted he should apply two different medicines to his eyes and demanded forty-five naira for the additional drop. He refused to give it, insisting that he owed no money to the hospital authorities, and demanded to see the doctor. It was then the right medicine was brought out and he was persuaded to go."

"That was one nurse out of the lot working there."

"But it happened all the same confirming my assertion that no facet of the society is corruption-proof. Before we ended our second round of debate, I promised I would work down the passion, I will give you more stunning instances. A middle-class officer in charge of students' affairs in a university in this country owns five cars. Most of his dupes are relieved of as much as fifteen thousand naira in order to put their names into the supplementary admission list. Whether or not they are flushed out later in their courses doesn't cost him a thought. Supplementary admission has now offered some university authorities a suspicion-free loop-hole for making money. Go to the public school system. How many principals on salary grade levels not terribly enviable have houses here and there, and change cars with incredible ease?"

"Mr. Igbokwe, come back to reality. These endless stories are nauseating. I hope you do feel the nausea."

"I don't know about nausea. I am not a medical man."

A waiter brought along a tray containing assorted drinks.

"What would you have sirs?"

Dr. Ume dropped his tumbler into the tray. "Mr. Igbokwe, I must be leaving. It is already past eleven. I hope to see you in better orientation some time somewhere."

"Good night Doc. and try to minimize attention to the ills of this country."

As the doctor drove home he wondered how insensitive his country men had become to moral and ethical issues. He began to soliloquise. We have enthroned falsehood, debauchery, graft, dishonesty, hypocrisy, irreligion and hedonism while trampling on charity, honesty, morality and greatness. To us greatness consists in possessing wealth only. As he thought deeply about Mr. Igbokwe's stiffness, his mind roved over a range of events. "Perhaps he thought, Mr. Igbokwe is right to a great extent. What I do not like is his intransigence, his total refusal to abjure what, two decades ago, he would stick out his neck for cutting rather than be associated with." He remembered a few incidents involving himself. He had written and sent four news talks to the state radio station for publication but none was read out. Two of them were mild attacks on obnoxious policies like demanding rent on dilapidated teachers' quarters and upholding wrong cultural practices which affected very important personalities in the state. It was a crime to throw a gibe at the sacred cows. A third one was an open letter to the newly elected local government chairmen in the country, suggesting what they should not do if they hoped to enjoy the confidence of their electors. "Perhaps if I flattered everybody, the news talks would have been read over and over again. This widespread hypocrisy can send one mad. As Mr. Igbokwe remarked: where does one start correcting these anomalies?"

Primary school teachers were already groaning with the pinch of poverty, having been owed for three months running. There were sporadic strike actions according to how each local government treated its teachers. In Ikpem Local Government Area, besides starving teachers of salaries for three months, their promotion, conversion and other arrears of payment and all sorts of allowances had been virtually written off as bad debts. Head teachers and classroom teachers who asked questions about them were marked out for castigation, intimidation and blackmail. Rather than lose all, the already famished teachers easily yielded to cheaply selling their consciences along with their rights. A handful of influential head teachers launched out to convince other head teachers that part of the arrears of payment had been paid some three months back, and insisted that the idea should be fed on to classroom teachers. "Meanwhile", they added, "the sympathetic secretary was relentlessly mounting pressure on the chairman to pay them two months' salaries at a go. If they continued embarrassing him with uncomplimentary questions, he might justifiably leave them to their fate."

Back at the different schools, the classroom teachers reacted spitefully. "Let them leave us to our fate. We have endured hunger for over three months. We have farms we can feed from. We shall have the three months' salary at a go or nothing. After getting the salaries, we start asking for the arrears." At an emergency meeting of the classroom teachers, it was agreed that any head teacher who got one kobo less than the target should be stoned.

At the local government secretariat, clerks and finance men were busy trumping up vouchers, figures and dates to vindicate the claim that some arrears of payment had been made even though one of their dates proved that the payment was made far ahead of the state government's approval of it.

One head teacher who could not understand the secretary's motive for waiving a federal government debt he was not required to pay with his own money, pitched a courageous battle with the whole secretariat.

"I am already in the bad books of everybody in this office; what name need I struggle to save by trying to please them? It is better I save it by winning the debate against them. The moment they retract the lie that some arrears of payment have been made, I will be prepared to lose the financial benefit. I simply want them, the pig-headed criminals, to be shamed. They have toyed enough with the destiny of teachers, and unless we say enough is enough, harder times await us."

Each time he went into the office to make enquiries about the secretary's directives or to get correct information about returns required by the office, spies walked hand-in-hand with him in the guise of enjoying his companionship, but he caught the joke early enough to maintain a safe distance as regards his remarks.

One of the lobbying head teachers, apparently friendly with the scape-goat was let loose on him. During his baited maiden visit to the uncompromising colleague, he tabled the topic.

"Mr. Oforka, aren't you yet convinced that we have got a sizeable part of our promotion and conversion arrears of payment?"

"I am not and will never be convinced because you right-hand men and your band of half-wits who have been drilled to re-echo their master's voice have no genuine figures or facts to back-up your argument. How can you convince even an idiot that the arrears of payment for which the state wing of the teachers' union had been engaged in unfriendly exchange of correspondence with the state Ministry of Education for over six months, and which the latter very reluctantly approved barely two months ago, was disbursed to the teachers in Ikpem Local Government Area of all local governments four months ago? When did the local government become so financially buoyant and so concerned about its teachers as to pay unapproved allowances when three months' salaries are being owed? I am afraid this is what happens when one's conscience is mortgaged. I used to have regard for you. Now you don't worth a kobo before me. Go and tell your secretary to sharpen his knife the more to make his lies more credible. Nobody is being deceived other than you and him."

The argument was too incontrovertible, forthright and poignant for the visitor to fumble a defence. The blot on his personal integrity immobilized his reasoning. He was both ashamed and embarrassed. He made some furtive effort to brighten up.

"Mr Oforka, you seem to have better information on this matter. Do you have up-to-date statistics to back up your assertions?"

"Yes, I have it. If you care to know the truth, come round and read my notes. He opened an exercise book he held firmly, giving the impression that he wouldn't part with it even for a split second.

Pretending to be studying it, Mr Ujara peered at it for about two minutes and said: "I cannot easily understand the statistics here and now. If you don't mind, bring it to the secretariat tomorrow. You and I will study it along with the accounts head who is inextricably involved in the financial matters of the education department."

"I don't have the energy or incentive to engage in extramural lessons for the accounts head or anybody else in that office for that matter. I have been vilified enough in that office to keep my distance. The best lesson they can have from me is renewed threat of having it out with them to any degree that they want it. Perhaps you might be good enough to relay my threat. The worst I expect is dismissal, and you can be sure I will leave office along with every Tom, Dick and Harry in that secretariat."

CHAPTER XII

Owing to strike actions now and then, the second term was hardly more than seven weeks of serious school work. The term therefore, dragged interminably, thus leaving the following vacation period a bare fortnight. Vero, like many other teachers, decided to spend it at home more for economic reasons than choice. Her mother fed her gratuitously as a demonstration of sympathy for non-payment of some months' salaries. Hardly a couple of days passed without her spending several hours at her station, ostensibly going to check for her salary. Mr. Ejema kept the appointment faithfully since it took place during office hours. Vero had a new suitor who lived three scores of kilometers away from her home.

"Vero," her mother called one morning as she was hurrying to leave for her station, "why don't you go and find out what is the matter with Ben who has not visited for more than three months, instead of making fruitless journeys to your station every other day?"

"I have no money for transport."

"How much is that? Your father can give it to you."

"I will not go. If he is serious he will call as often as possible."

"You don't allow for illness and other inconveniences."

"I say I am not going. Is he the only man on earth?"

"Please don't bite off my head. I mean well."

"Enough of your concern! You cannot choose a man for me."

Her father followed the trend of altercation without intervening for the sake of propriety. To keep children out of ear-shot, Michael, Vero's father invited his wife to his bedroom shortly after Vero had left.

"Have you noticed the dramatic change in Vero's attitude to Ben in the last two months?" he asked tersely. "This holiday period has given me an insight into her mode of life. I strongly suspect that a certain man must be pulling wool over her eyes. Daughters confide more in their mothers than their fathers especially in matters regarding marriage. It will pay off well if you humorously tease her with marriage. Her reaction will prove me right or wrong."

"That is a good observation, Michael. I have the same suspicion but I held my breath because women are regarded as not giving a second thought before voicing their feelings. Veronica never spoke so boldly to me. When Ben called on the first day, he was second to no suitor. Now in her scale, he is as good as any other man. Let us cross our fingers and watch the development. If I tease her she will chop off my head."

"Silently watching the development would not be a safe measure. Women have a period in their development when they have a spate of marriage offers. If that period passes, their engagement is fraught with difficulty. Besides, once a woman is associated with some scandal, her eventual marriage becomes a remote affair. Let us head off the obstacle before it takes root. Talk to her. If she proves aggressive, I add my weight."

"I will do all I can."

"Do it as soon as possible – before this holidays ends".

Mr. Ejeme gave Vero anything just for the asking. Their illicit association was now an open secret, and gossips capitalized on it. Mr. Ejeme's wife was torn between reacting violently, thereby aggravating her husband's diminishing image among teachers, and continued indulgence at the risk of flagrant derision from her social inferiors. Her husband was artfully balancing the delicate situation. At home he never mentioned Vero.

If, fortuitously, the matter cropped up, he took a quasi self-righteous and aggressive stance and followed it up with projecting an undeservedly pitiable position that disgruntled and frustrated teachers castigate him for no reason, in spite of his candid efforts to ameliorate their hardship. But his frequent late returning to his house in the recent months eroded the uneasy peace prevailing in his residence.

Juli went from one room to another, looking for what exactly she didn't know. The shrill cry of her little daughter, apparently hit by her elder sister, impinged on her distraught mind and she bounced out of the house blindly but the miscreants were not within easy reach.

"What is happening, Ify?"

"Mma hit me on the face."

"Mma, report here before I get at you."

"She has run away."

"Let her run to wherever. She will later return home."

"She re-entered the living room and sat on a long settee. The uneasiness assumed fresh vehemence. It verged on insanity. Taking a decision was unimaginable when the seat of reason was racked. At school that afternoon, her husband had been the subject of general discussion. In spite of her presence, the secretary's clandestine association with Vero was x-rayed and analysed like the result of a science experiment.

"What does the secretary see in this loafer that makes him sacrifice his honour and domestic peace?"

"It is unbelievable; how mean; how foolhardy!"

"Doesn't he know that the girl has a serious suitor?"

"The girl herself should use her discretion if she is worthy of any man's serious attention."

"You talk as if you are not a woman", one of them challenged the last speaker. "In these days of 'work and no pay', anyone who provides a spinster's needs is her dearest. Even married women hardly resist the temptation; what more spinsters?"

"Granted but she should know that her paramour is a married man whose wife has a right to be jealous. Would she tolerate that degree of appropriation if her husband was so transplanted from her home?"

"I am afraid women are always easy targets. The man should be more sensible than that. How many married men have no mistresses outside? If carefully managed, a wife would bet that her husband never spoke to any other woman."

These excruciating remarks invaded her mind with such pungency that waiting patiently for his return became an extra-ordinary ordeal. Yet she had no other rational option. She went to bed to coax sleep but that effort was worse than futile.

Vero intuitively thought she was having her last chance for a long time to come. She introduced one frivolous topic after another in order to delay Mr Ejeme's leaving that evening.

"Sir, what will your wife feel like if I visit your house?"

"Never imagine that. Our affair is no longer a secret. My wife has on more than one occasion mentioned it to me but with masculine braggadocio I brushed it aside."

"Will she fight me if I come?"

"She will do anything you can't imagine and I will side with her. She is my lawful wife."

"Dismiss that thought from your mind. I am a Christian in the first place. Secondly I wouldn't like to increase my economic burden."

"But for the church thing I would love to be your second wife. If people of your status in life complain of economic burden, what will people in the grips of stark poverty say, and they have families, in many cases large ones?"

"Why all this prattle? I thought you told me you had an intended husband. I hope he hasn't jilted you."

"Jilting? It's rather I who intend to jilt him. He doesn't appear serious".

"Don't let go so easily. Good husbands are not easy to come by".

"What makes him a good husband? We haven't started living together".

"What fault then disqualifies him?"

"For more than three months he hasn't visited us nor written a letter".

"That is a test of fidelity. The loop-hole he has given will prove you serious or whimsical. If he doesn't come, why don't you go to find out what keeps him away from you?"

"Mother has suggested that but I do not want to give the impression that I need him badly otherwise he will bluff me when we get married."

"I've got to go now. My wife must be terribly uneasy."

"Sir, what about these arrears of salaries owed to us? Your office doesn't seem to give them a thought."

"That's quite wrong. Something is being done about teachers' salaries. Machinery has been set up to work out modalities for piece-meal payment of the arrears along with current months salaries."

"I don't understand your big language. When shall we have any payment at all?"

"Not too far from now. See you again in a few days' time."

When Mr. Ejeme returned home, Juli was literally boiling with anger.

"Why is the room so dark? Children, where is your mummy?"

"She is in the bedroom", replied Mma.

"I hope she is well. Why does she choose to be in a dark room?" Has National Electric Power Authority (N.E.P.A) cut off power to our compound?"

"No sir, there is light in the kitchen."

He stepped into the living room and turned on the light, and walked into the bedroom. "Juli, why do you continue siesta till so late? I hope you are well". There was no response.

"What is the matter?"

"Don't disturb anybody. Go back to your office and tidy up everything."

"Who told you I was in the office all the while?"

"Where else could you be till so late?" She sat up now.

"I had to see a number of friends."

"It were better you continued the itinerary endlessly."

"What an effrontery. I know your mentors have filled your empty head with silly ideas. You must give credence to every idle gossip."

"Your intelligent head has over-reached itself and made you a laughing stock in this town."

"You exposed me to ridicule. Nobody knows my so called weakness but you."

"Shame faced pretence. You exposed yourself beyond covering up."

"I have had enough of that impudence."

"You cannot have too much of it since you put no value on dignity of family, dignity of office or respect for your marriage vows."

"Do my marriage vows enjoin that I should make myself a hermit?"

"They give you a licence to be way-ward."

"I say enough of that provocation. It is in your interest not to push me to the limit of endurance. You have taken enough liberty with my endurance".

"Your threats harden my resolve to salvage what remains of your personality before you lapse into oblivion."

"You can be next to the commissioner for education yet you allow animal passion to becloud your reasoning faculty. Who is this Vero of a woman who moulds you like putty? The day I will set my eyes on her, she will forever regret knowing you."

"There you are. I knew you had been brain-washed by the despicable gossips whose stock-in-trade is tale bearing."

"Gossip is a common human foible. Only weak human beings fall victim to it. For a sensible person it has a salutary effect."

Mr. Ejeme decided to drop the matter because his children were getting interested, trying to move into the bedroom to watch them. Juli sensed the same and reciprocated the gesture.

That night, Vero arrived home so late that the impropriety could not fail to attract comments from her parents. As soon as she changed her dress, her mother went into her room.

"Vero, did you go to see Ben today?"

"I am sick of Ben. Possibly he has bribed you."

"Bribed me to do what? Persuade you to marry him? This is childish. I am happily settled in my husband's home. You want to make yourself a vamp. You will surely need a husband when you cannot have one."

"At my age and with my training, I can fend for myself."

"Who sponsored your training? You have so soon forgotten the property we had to sell in order to provide your needs in college. Do you need any prompting to show gratitude to your parents"?

"Sponsoring my education wasn't an extraordinary favour. Every other couple does it for their children..."

"Who, in turn, provide them with basic comfort when they start working."

"For how long have I worked? How much do you think I earn monthly?"

"My daughter, small as you think earnings are, a sensible, well-meaning man will keep you comfortable if you live a virtuous life."

Vero was unable to continue the argument, having been disarmed by a sense of guilt and suppressed remorse.

Vero's only female confidant, Hilda, got Ben's postal address from her friend's room. Ostensibly intending to stem the tide of rumour mongering and detraction threatening her friend's nuptial voyage, Hilda wrote a letter to Ben who knew her by proxy. The writer's postal or contact address was intentionally withheld.

Dear Ben,

You certainly will wonder who is writing you. I am Hilda, Vero's close friend and confident. You and I must have been introduced to each other in absentia by means of pictures. Disturbed by the web of scandal and criticism which my friend has spun around herself, I am moved by genuine concern for the safety of her marriage proposal to give you early information with a view to inciting prompt intervention from you if you seriously intend to marry her. She and the education secretary here have enmeshed themselves so scandalously that neither has a name left to protect. The secretary's wife is after her life.

I hope you will give this signal the priority it deserves.

Lots of love from

Hilda.

Having read the letter, Ben reclined on his sofa, pensively trying to recall the memory of Hilda. He remembered going through Vero's picture album some six months back and seeing two ladies in the same fabric tailored in the same fashion, one of them being Vero. Discerning anxiety on his face, Vero nipped the budding question by introducing the other lady as "My bosom friend, Hilda, a fellow teacher". Taking a deep breath, he sat up to scrutinise the altruistic genuineness of this interference. If the intention of this letter wasn't vicious, the writer's address would have been inserted. "Does this meddler think I am such a juvenile that I am ignorant of love intrigue rife among unmarried ladies who will go any length in undoing very cordial friends to get an advantage to themselves?"

That rhetorical reasoning seemed to give him a respite to smile at the seeming mischief. He tucked the letter away in his table drawer.

After supper he relaxed once more on his sofa. The theme of the letter besieged him anew. The mist of passionate bias in favour of Vero began to disperse gradually. Women could be fickle. Could Vero interpret my relatively long absence as a sign of coldness? A feeling of guilt seemed to get the better of him. Then he continued his silent rhetorical questioning. Are eligible young men so numerous that within a space of three months a girl can transfer her avowed love entirely to another suitor, what more to a supposedly responsible married man? Possibly Hilda is employing a ruse to divert attention to herself or at worst ruin her friend's chances so that both remain spinsters, but the letter implicates a local dignitary who would not put up with calumny. He was hard put to it apportioning blame.

Now he had taken a hard look at the letter, a more difficult problem surfaced: what appropriate action could he take in the face of the confusion? He stumbled on the only plausible option. The following morning he put in for one week's casual leave "to enable me to straighten out things at home". Being the first of its kind since he started work in the department, the application was successful.

He traveled straight to Vero's school and was informed she had been transferred to another town. Although the new station was a familiar place, he decided to visit her parents first. The meeting caused mutual embarrassment. Her parents were hearing of the transfer for the first time. Little evidence was required to vindicate Hilda's allegation. He didn't know Hilda's school but even if he knew it, it would appear immature making a breathless enquiry into the allegation soon after returning home. He calmly returned to his house to let off the steam before taking any other line of action. In spite of everything, he was perfectly in control of his emotion.

He had sound sleep at night and rose early to map out his strategy. The most sensible step, in his opinion, was to find out how long ago she was transferred to her new station. Returning to her former school, he went straight to the head teacher who never met him before, introduced himself and made the enquiry.

"Are you engaged to Vero?"

"Yes."

"I see. The transfer letter came barely three weeks ago but she was still here until the middle of last week. Where do you livel?"

"At Enugu. I am on one week's leave."

"If you must see her, better go to Ife Community Primary School before the closing hour – 1.45 pm."

"Thank you very much. I am going to the place right away". His mental alertness and presence of mind were such that he forgot nothing that needed exploration.

"Before I forget sir, do you know any teacher by name Hilda?"

"What is her surname?"

"I don't know. All I know is that she is Vero's friend."

"I see. I remember the girl. I don't know where she teaches but I will find out in a minute."

He sent for one of the lady teachers who told them that she was teaching at Amaichi Primary School.

As he was walking to the end he pondered the clause, "If you must see her". "This conditional clause must be preposterous if it has no ugly connotation. At every turn there is an element of surprise and concealed disappointment. I was rash in imputing motives about Hilda's letter."

He arrived at Amachi Primary School a few minutes to one o'clock and Hilda was about signing off. On seeing him she rushed out of the head teacher's office to forestall any enquiry about her. She ran to him and embraced him.

"Did you receive my letter?"

"Yes but it has neither date nor contact address. I would have been here much earlier if I knew where you were."

"I am sorry. I was terribly in a hurry. Let's go to my house. It is not too far from here."

They walked the two odd kilometers, exchanging pleasantries, Hilda asking funny questions about Enugu.

In her one-room apartment, she offered him the only chair available. "Make yourself comfortable on the chair, please. I hope you are not in a hurry. You must eat something before leaving, having come a long way from Enugu".

"No, I returned home yesterday. I am coming from my home. Where is your friend?"

"Haven't you seen her?"

"No, I don't know where she is."

"How did you know my school?"

"I got information from her former school."

"Please may I take leave of you for a short while. I will re-join you in less than fifteen minutes". She pushed a photo album to him.

In about twenty minutes she had prepared some food big enough for one person.

"Please ignore my poor cooking. I was hurrying to save you time."

"Tremendous generosity to someone you never saw before."

Not at all sir. Although we are meeting for the first time, I have known much about you. Vero has told me a lot about you."

"Yes, where is Vero?"

"You mean she hasn't informed you of her transfer or are you playing pranks? Men can pretend much better than women."

"I am very frank. Would it make sense my coming here?"

"She is at Ife Community Primary School. I hope you are familiar with the town."

"Certainly but I don't intend to go there right away. She will wonder how I knew her whereabouts since she has informed neither me nor her parents. I called on them yesterday and they expressed embarrassing surprise at my mentioning her transfer."

"God forbid. Vero has acted most unwisely."

"I wonder why she chooses to maintain secrecy about it."

Hilda chuckled. "She knows better. For public servants transfer is a routine exercise and doesn't entail secrecy."

"Possibly she wants to escape from the scandal you mentioned in your letter but that wouldn't be a very effective measure since secrecy makes room for suspicion and wild allegations."

"Please don't quote me. The secretary will bear me hard. I wrote the letter with good intentions. I never intended disparaging my friend or the secretary."

"But it is a topical issue in the local government area. Her former head teacher's sneer spoke volume. I take it in the same spirit as you do, and I hope you will oblige me with details. That will enable me to take important decisions."

"I hope you are not contemplating ending your engagement to Vero."

"By no means. If you throw more light on the issue, I will be better able to work out a strategy to end the slushy relationship."

"Ben, I will not lie to you. Vero has cut a sorry figure for herself. I don't know whether she and the secretary took a love potion together. None can bear the other's absence for a couple of days. The licentious fraternizing threatened the secretary's marriage so much that he resorted to what he stupidly thought was a safe measure, and Vero lost her reason in the voluptuous indulgence. She doesn't need to be told that she is toying with a man whose education, religion and social standing rule out polygamy."

"Thank you very much, Hilda. I have a week's leave beginning yesterday. I will try and see her tomorrow probably."

"Please if you do go, don't give her the impression that you have seen me otherwise I will be made a scape goat for the circulation of the scandalous story."

"You can rely on my good sense. I will never mention you at all. Good bye."

"Bye and safe journey back to Enugu."

Ben had a frank chat with his parents that night and their decision was to call it quits with Vero's people. He returned to Enugu the following day.

"Vero's transfer saved the secretary and his wife a lot of embarrassment in the vicinity of their living quarters. The theatre of licentious drama was removed to safe quarters while rehearsal constancy was almost eliminated. Vero did not lose common-sense completely in spite of her promiscuity. The secretary had told her point-blank times without number that he would, on no condition, take a second wife. She now decided to make virtue out of necessity: ensure maximum material gain from the secretary and court an eligible young man with the gifts. She was sick of uncomplimentary publicity. In a neighbouring local government area, she spied charming Willie who derived joy from turning down gestures from would-be wives. Willie always fell in love at first sight but got fed up with equal ease. With Vero there seemed to be a positive reversal of trend. On her part, Vero tactfully withheld mention of the secretary and very rarely invited Willie to her station unless on the occasion she was dead sure that the secretary would not visit. Willie had a present every other month: Shirts, handkerchiefs, wrist watches, sandals, besides food stuffs which were a regular feature in the relationship.

With Willie giving in absolutely to Vero's wishes the latter had little reason to regret losing Ben but she was very reluctant to inform her parents of her new find. They had already discounted her from the scheme of things in their family.

"Would you like to know my parents?" Vero asked Willie one day as their conversation covered a whole range of topics.

"Why not if you invite me?"

"I would love to but I don't like to whip up sentiment in my parents and their neighbours once more."

"Once more? Have you been engaged to anyone before?"

"Briefly to one civil servant who was too timid to declare his interest. When I noticed that, I gave him the boot. I believe you will make a good husband. Your love is whole and entire. You are a handsome, bold, young man. One feels proud walking side-by-side with you. You are superbly fashionable".

"I have to confess, I never was so attached to a woman", reacted Willie. "It had been head over heels in love today and antagonism the next month. Let us allow the mutual feeling of affection to take root in us before disclosing our engagement to people. Perhaps I failed with others because the "parading" couldn't stand social limelight. My parents want me to simply declare genuine interest in some girl; the whole burden of marriage expenses will be borne by them."

"I feel persuaded to reciprocate your forthrightness. We are both adults, so denying certain things will be either mean or dishonest. The education secretary in my local government area is a very delightful man. But for his being married I would have gone to any length with him. Do not be discouraged; we have long ended our affairs but we remain acquaintances. He is too sensible and compassionate to put my marriage in jeopardy when I spared his."

"Never mind; we must allow for youthful exuberance provided it doesn't carry over into the future."

"I will not hesitate to take an oath against that. I should start thinking of my own family."

These declarations would be reliable oaths if human nature safeguarded absolute honesty. It takes extraordinary virtue and often strong will-power in fair women to be completely faithful especially when old acquaintance is baited with liberal presents. Vero kept widely-spaced but regular dates with the secretary.

"If I get seriously attached to another suitor, will you still visit me?" Vero asked Mr. Ejeme one day.

"If you so wish. I love your company but I am beginning to feel that I am an obstacle to your marriage. Have you really jettisoned Ben?"

"Long ago. He is not the type of person I will live happily with."

"Well, for a group-up man or woman, the choice of a life partner is an individual's exclusive responsibility as distinct from child betrothal which parents do for their children. In any case, be tactful. If you pick and drop constantly, the moment rumour goes round that you are choosy, unmarried men will keep their distance."

"They can go and hang. Am I getting so old in appearance that I should rush the choice?"

"By no means but, unlike men, women have a peak period for getting marriage overtures after which they will depend on luck or lose taste."

"Every man or woman has ideals which guide marriage choice. It would be irrational if one throws those over-board in order to catch up with the peak period. It is better to remain unmarried for long than hurry only to regret it shortly. Divorce is everything but complimentary for a woman."

"I am afraid you are rationalizing too much about marriage. The so-called ideals are never complete in one man or woman. Often times marriages based on a lucky dip turn out to be more pleasurable than those riddled with choice. There is an element of luck in marriage. By and large, the sooner you start giving marriage a serious thought the better."

"I have taken the advice, nevertheless if you have had enough of my company, say it point blank. I should be grateful to you for keeping up our friendship in spite of tale-bearing and your wife's reactions."

"Who tells you about my wife's reaction?"

"We don't live in a lonely island. My fellow female teachers sometimes gossip to my hearing but I have always pitched my hope on your reliable constancy."

"I wouldn't be a good friend if I selfishly enjoyed our relationship without giving a damn about your future happiness which I can't guarantee. As regards my wife, she is not the gullible type. She sieves every rumour affecting my family before accepting it as true or rejecting it. I never gave her the loop-hole to attach importance to rumour or gossip."

"I was pulling your feet. My intention was to inform you informally that I have spotted an agreeable young man but we haven't made our intention known to anybody even my confidant, Hilda, although I no longer feel safe in her company. She hasn't paid me a visit since my transfer here. Chances are that she has joined the band of self-righteous critics who see me as trying to dispossess your wife of you."

"Don't mistrust her. She might prove a friend in deed after all."

When Vero visited home next, everything seemed to give her cold shoulders. There was no pet dog frisking around her. She later learnt with indignation that it had been sold. There was nobody around to give her information about the whereabouts of members of her family. She loitered dejectedly and fumbled unsuccessfully at several niches for the key to the living room. She had ambled round the compound several times, peeping into every nook and cranny without any set objective, before her youngest brother returned.

"Sylva where did you go?"

"To pick pear at 'Uhu' from where we moved to here."

"Give me the key please. Where did Papa go?"

"I don't know. He left here early in the morning on his bicycle."

"What about Mama?"

"She went to Ubo to visit a woman who gave birth to a baby last week."

On gaining entry into her mother's room, she went straight into the kitchen which served the dual purpose of kitchen and pantry.

"Sylva, why is there no foodstuff left here?"

"I don't know. Only mother can answer that question."

She slumped in a cushioned chair in utter disappointment. It was mid afternoon before her mother returned. She greeted her with a pitch-dark face and she responded in a similar mood.

"Where did they say you went?"

"To see Ibeji who nearly lost her life in the labour of her last child".

She made some attempt to brighten up a little but the load of all-round disappointment weighed heavily on her. She summoned courage to trigger off the commotion.

"Why is there no bit of foodstuff here? I hope you are not starving yourselves in the name of austerity."

"Yes, we are. We expected you would have some feeling for the old couple you left at home who have no regular income. Perhaps you brought us some food items or money."

"I brought you my head. Are the times so hard that you had to sell Rubby the wonderful watchdog?"

"What was it watching for us? What do we have to lose to thieves when we can't afford a decent meal for ourselves?

"You had no sympathy for a pet dog that had lived with you for several years."

"You are funny. Would you prefer it died of hunger? If we can't feed ourselves, what excess shall we leave for the dog?"

"You should have sent me words to come and remove it."

"How would we contact you? By the way, where are you now?"

"My failure to inform you is reason enough for you to treat me so coldly?"

"I don't know what you mean by cold treatment."

"You will know when you choose. I arrived here in the morning. It hasn't occurred to you to ask whether I would taste anything. Have you grown many times poorer since I visited home last; a sudden famine indeed."

"Have you seen Ben recently? He came here to find out your whereabouts but we couldn't help him when he mentioned your transfer. He made us know of it. I thought he knew your new station before visiting us."

"I was wondering when you would mention Ben. I believe my real offence against everybody in this house is not encouraging Ben. Other offences are either imagined or trumped up to bolster the sacrilege I committed."

"Maybe your conscience is passing sentence on you. Who said you committed a sacrilege? Who charged you with not encouraging Ben? The last time I mentioned him to you, you said you were grown-up enough to fend for yourself. That day we left you alone to take care of yourself. If not for the transfer thing, I can hardly think of anything that would make me mention him again to you."

"Sincere enough, that ends the matter. However, as your mother I am bound to give advice for your safety. Whether you take it or not is another question. Now you have bidden Ben good-bye, be careful of yourself. A single young woman is exposed to danger all round. Control your association with men, otherwise you risk not getting married at all. We were three girls from my mother's house, today all of us are married. Michael will be the last man to tolerate a grown-up daughter sharing his house with him."

"Good gracious! What put this silly idea into your head? Did you go round looking for men before Michael picked you up? You wanted to know my new station so as to bother me with marriage sermons every day. I repeat, enough of your concern. I can take care of myself. If you see me here again, call me a bastard."

"I wouldn't indict myself calling you that."

"Then call me a thief."

As they were bandying words, her father rode in.

"Who is that exchanging words with you, Adaugo?"

"It is Vero, her mother's co-wife."

"She will not be your co-wife in my house. She had better get her own husband and say what she likes in his house."

Picking up her bag, she said: "Good bye, if you see me here again, give me the worst curse parents can give a daughter."

"You have already cursed yourself. We will not add to it", replied her father.

CHAPTER XIII

Local government chairmen were caught off guard by the sudden dissolution of local government councils. The governor followed up the action with setting up panels to probe the alleged financial imprudence of chairmen in local government areas where the allegation was most rampant. The chairman of Ikpem Local Government was one of the victims. Since no chairman has time to piece loose ends together, it wasn't easy for them to co-ordinate lying or to cook the books. The panel unearthed a lot of irregularities in the funds meant for education. The most incriminating offence was the fact that notwithstanding arrears of salaries owed teachers, the figures quoted in the salary budgets were far above the maximum necessary to offset every expense in the education department.

The education secretary and every member of the local government finance staff were implicated and subjected to brain-racking questioning. When Vero asked her friend about the progress and possible implications of the probe, he answered: "I was only an errand boy. The chairman was the chief executive of the council and should be answerable for all the financial irregularities of the council."

"What about irregular payment of teachers' salaries which seemed to be your responsibility?"

"I was only a pay master. If he ordered payment, I would effect that, otherwise I maintained that funds were not available."

"Let us hope that you will get away unscathed."

The secretary knew that he was everything but an errand boy. The statement was a palliative for embarrassment. The fear of danger which haunted the pair provided an undesirable holiday from their wonted meeting. Naturally the scale of contact was tilted in favour of Willie who in spite of the unabated allurement, was becoming uneasy about the obstructionist tendency of the secretary. After an ingenious maneuver by the adroit coordinator to accommodate an old timer and financier without estranging the possible object of future happiness, Willie had the feeling that the game was up and that continued silence would amount to imbecility. The contract was too fragile to survive cuckolding him so early. The fastness had to be discredited if they were not to build on a foundation of pretence. Before he decided on how to approach the matter, the receding hateful interference of the unequal competitor coupled with the apparently increased inclination of Vero to his side had weakened his resolve to blow open the deception. On the other hand, what did he have to lose in an association he did very little of the spending necessary to sustain it? Nonetheless, his parents had seen him so often in the company of Vero that they were entertaining hopes of an eventual permanent union between them, and he felt it was time he gave up perching on girls.

The unspoken mind of Willie made a perceptible appearance in the form of occasional brusque reaction to Vero's suggestions or approaches which might have passed without a hint of disapproval when enthusiasm hadn't been mitigated by suspicion. The once welcome, if wanton, frolicsomeness on the part of Vero now appeared excessive to Willie. This attitude wasn't lost on Vero, yet the force pulling her to the secretary was doubly insurmountable. She had noticed symptoms of pregnancy and wanted to pull a fast one on both men but she was restrained by lack of opportunity to move out as often as she desired, since

Willie's visits appeared unpredictable and often ill-timed in her view. Meetings with the secretary became painfully rarer, yet she was relentlessly looking for a possible chance to exploit.

On one of such rare occasions, when a reunion was safely possible, Vero decided to make a clean breast of the whole matter to Mr. Ejeme. Just before they parted ways, she announced between smiling and frowning: "Secretary, I am carrying a three-month old pregnancy for you."

The secretary squirmed instantly, "That is unfortunate. You don't have to say it a second time."

"I am not kidding you. Have I cracked such a joke with you before?"

The secretary's appearance became more repellant. "You informed me you had been engaged to a man for marriage. Isn't it possible he is responsible for the pregnancy?"

"It is I alone who know the father of my unborn baby."

"I doubt the reliability of that knowledge. Knowledge can be a mere opinion; it can be wishful thinking; it can be fallacious; there are a thousand and one fancies that can pass for knowledge. It depends on the aims or wishes of the one claiming possession of it."

Resolved to match seriousness with bluntness, Vero shouted. "I can't understand what you mean. Check your utterances or I take my life here and now before you. Oh

I should have known that in this sort of association, the woman is always the loser."

The secretary actually passed out. Why should this benumbing coincidence visit him now? He would have protested if he had enough soberness and control of his nerves. A film of tears shielded his eyes from Vero's piercing stare. For the first time in his dare-devil escapade, the hell which is his house was dawned on him. The noose which he inadvertently tied around his neck was getting tighter every second. He surrendered to implacable fate. Betrayed by a conspiracy of eventualities, rejected by his humiliated and almost abandoned wife, haunted by fear of disgorging a yet unimaginable sum of money which he kept in safety nowhere, he resolved to sign a temporary truce with fate.

"Vero," he pleaded in a mellowed tone, "I didn't mean to wound your feeling. I have always expressed my desire to see you well married, and thought that since you have a serious suitor, the pregnancy could be made to appear his responsibility. Perhaps you never knew what I am going through. Even if I discarded all principle and decide to have you as my second wife, neither you no I can survive the storm my wife will great us with. Please I will make any reasonable financial contribution required of me to keep you comfortable before and after delivery provided you completely absolve me of that act.

Vero was overwhelmed with sympathy for a chum who had been beset with difficulties she immensely contributed to. She sobbed pathetically, whether in sympathy for her own precarious state she alone knew.

The probe had taken a dramatic, though foreseeable, turn against the secretary. The chairman had a very strong alibi. He insisted, "I am neither an educationist nor a trained financial administrator. I therefore relied on the expert advice of my education secretary. I gave him free rein to control the finances of the education department.

The drowning secretary summoned what was left of his manliness to pay the chairman a visit a day after an unusually long session at which the secretary was stretched almost to breaking point. On seeing the chairman, he broke down and started shedding tears. The chairman was too hardened by the desire to safeguard self to be affected by what appeared to him as an indiscrete display of incompetence. He saw him merely as not smart enough in the diplomacy of self-preservation. Sympathy could justifiably be waived in the mean time.

Between feminine sobs the secretary mumbled: "Sir you treated me like this though i was prepared to do your bidding often against my inclination. You would love to see me crucified for an offence you know I was only an obedient accomplice."

Mr. Ejeme, the chairman dispassionately rejoined, "no matter your feeling, you have to appreciate my difficulty. I was a victim of a hopeless dilemma: speak the truth and get my good friend in trouble or tell lies in sympathy and have myself roped in. If you were in my situation, you would have done no better, I am afraid."

"You believe you spoke the whole truth. Heaven is my witness."

"I am no less a Christian. My first responsibility to myself is preserving my own life. The second is not to threaten anybody else's own."

"Thank you. Truth can be only momentarily suppressed, it cannot be destroyed. One day it will surface. Good night."

"Willie dear, I am afraid you are no longer the pliable Willie I cherished. I have noticed of late that you are indifferent to my presence, unconcerned about my mood and unconcerned about my health complaints. Please tell me my faults and I will make amends if really they are the matter. Starve me of food but show sympathy with my changing moods. You were at my station last week-end. Your arrival coincided with my return from my home where I had a painful brush with my parents. The signs were too manifest on my face to be covered up, yet they elicited no sympathy or concern from you. This afternoon I have stayed with you for over one hour without noticing a smile or a genuine feeling of care in you. It is make-belief all through."

The passionate appeal coupled with the usual feminine resort, lavish tears, conjured up the desired effect. Willie immediately succumbed in spite of himself.

Vero, I am at a loss of words. How would I know you had a clash with your parents? You simply transferred the aggression to me, hence you saw apathy where it never existed. When you complained about not feeling well, my advice was that you should see a doctor since you did not really know what it was. Was that not concern enough? Whatever be the case, I am sorry if I fell short of your expectations. Tears are most unwelcome now please." He took her in his arms and she yielded quickly to his warm embrace.

With confidence in Willie re-instated, Vero was emboldened. "Willie, I had a fancy this week. When are we going to start marriage formalities?"

"You have not introduced me to your parents yet. Where do we start?" Definitely marriage is never an exclusive affair between two lovers. On my side, my anxious parents must have drawn some conclusions without being re-assured by anybody."

"If I am right, a couple of over twenty-one years can marry without their parent's consent. Suppose we met overseas, couldn't we have married without informing our parents?"

"I admire your mature reasonableness in this affair and, in fact, love you the more for it but perhaps you need to be better informed about my peculiar circumstance before you make up your mind on your stance. I rejected my first suitor against my parent's wish, and they vowed never to welcome any other one. I wouldn't like to take you to hostile parents. Perhaps when time and the arrival of a baby heal the wound, they will be better disposed to receive us. I hope I am not reasoning like an inexperienced girl."

"Far from that, I never thought you were capable of such sedate thinking, but we shall have stiff opposition from my own parents. They will never sanction our wedding without coming into formal contact with their fellow parents-in-law. May be you will have the task of getting them won over to your point of view. The very fact that the idea comes from you exposes you to suspicion before them."

"Dear, spare me the charge of obstinate insistence for I have problems all round. I am bearing a three-month old pregnancy for you." At once, she switched the searchlight of her eyes onto Willie's face.

Willie went out of his way to camouflage his loss of poise.

"That is a much lighter matter than the first problem. A couple can wed after getting children. That needn't cause any embarrassment in an environment like ours where emphasis in marriage is on procreation. We can say without blame that we wanted to test our fertility before committing ourselves to life partnership."

"Let us sleep over it, Willie. We might stumble on better ideas in the near future." She felt re-assured of the much desired rapport.

That evening when Vero left, Willie went on journey down memory lane. Much as he had been reckless in his affairs with women, he found no tangible reason to indict himself now. Vero had always insisted on her safe period and he had always obliged her. What prevented her from informing him of this much earlier in spite of their constant exchange of visits? Who knows what caused the alleged friction between her and her parents? Above all, in the last two months or so, she had not insisted on her safe period. The moodiness and unprovoked irritability had explained themselves, he felt. If she had nothing to hide, she would have taken interest in announcing it as soon as she noticed it. He had two options: accept responsibility without protest and forget all about marriage proceedings since native custom forbids such rites until the baby is delivered; or make his feelings about the pregnancy known to her and reject responsibility for it whatever the consequences on the delicate sensibilities of the double-faced vamp.

Wouldn't it be necessary to confide in his father? The chances were that his father would encourage accepting the pregnancy, for the child when born, wouldn't choose a father, neither would a third party know of the quandary surrounding it. His father had no idea of the surreptitious dealings with the secretary. His head swarmed with conflicting ideas. His mental agony was made more acute by the fact that Vero got closer and closer to him now. She spent more days at his station than hers, thereby missing school a good number of days in a month without fear of query from her head teacher or secretary who was grappling with his own problem.

He thought of consulting his close male associates since young men had identical sexual problems and were always prepared to help out one another, but that would amount to publicizing a secret yet between him and a person he might eventually marry. If he was going to reject responsibility for the pregnancy, the sooner he did it, the better, as belated action could have dangerous consequences on the expectant mother. On sober reflections he began to wonder what had converted him into a very mild fellow in the hands of Vero. How many girls in the same plight had he thrown off without any compunction or after effect? An answer provided itself readily: was that positive victory in the real sense?

The last day Mr. Ejeme was arraigned before the probing panel, he tried to shelter himself with the same argument which seemed to have given the chairman partial or total reprieve. His defence shifted the guilt to his accounts head whom he presented as the architect of the whole misappropriation.

"I am a professional educationist. I have no knowledge of accounting. We entirely depended on the guidance and figures presented by the accounts head".

"But you gave directives sir," replied the nervous finance officer when the panel directed him to cross-examine the secretary.

"How could you take directives not backed up with professional expertise? Don't you reserve the right to turn down any directive you find likely to draw you to financial risk?"

Technically the defence was quite sound and would have created a new scape-goat if the god of retribution had not induced the panel chairman to glance at some of the documents recovered from the secretary's office.

"Gentlemen", he appealed, "I have a few questions for the bursar, whatever you call him. Mr. bursar please, since you took charge of finance in this department, have you been audited by state auditors?"

"Yes sir, two or three times."

"Was the secretary interviewed or questioned by the team"

"No sir, all the questions were directed to me and I did the necessary clarification and tendered documents for inspection."

"What lesson did you learn from that?"

"That I would be held responsible for any money unaccounted for."

Then he pushed one of the vouchers he was studying to him and asked: whose signature is that?

He examined it carefully and said, "Not mine sir."

He turned to the secretary. "Mr. secretary, who signed that voucher?"

"I never signed any salary vouchers. What I signed was salary bill prepared by the accounts department."

"Bursar, does any of your finance clerks sign salary vouchers?"

"No sir, that is my exclusive responsibility."

"Gentlemen, it appears there are ghost workers in this office. We have reached a crucial stage in our inquiry. If we clear the mystery surrounding these vouchers, we have struck at the heart of the matter. There are about fifteen vouchers here bearing the same or almost the same signature."

"Where were they recovered from?" asked a member of the panel. The panel secretary cross-checked their serial numbers with the inventory he compiled on the day those documents were collected and said, "from the secretary's office."

"Mr. secretary", the chairman resumed, you ought to explain the mystery about those fictitious signatures. It appears to me that you have a private bursar who signs very confidential vouchers for you."

The secretary stammered something incomprehensible and swallowed hard with his gaze fixed on the floor of the room.

"Secretary to the panel, see whether there are any other vouchers in your file."

He heaved up two fat files and flipped through the first one. "Yes sir, there are."

"Where did we remove them from?"

"The Accounts-Head's office."

"Compare the dates on the two sets."

He bent down over the files containing them, arranged each group in date serial order before doing the comparison.

"Sir, the correspondence in dates points to duplication but the figures vary disproportionately. The figures on the apocryphal vouchers are a lot bigger than those on the authenticated ones."

"Apocryphal indeed," remarked the chairman humorously. You Scripture Union folks! Anyone who has financial dealings with you must be extra-careful".

Turning to the education secretary, he asked, "Mr. Secretary, do you want us to believe that you are ignorant of the signatory to these vouchers?"

There was no response, and the panel adjourned for two days.

On the day the panel wound up its assignment, the secretary took the team to a hotel for relaxation. The business-like attitude and thoroughness of the panel discouraged any attempt to talk business, in the local parlance, with them. However, he managed to slip a fat envelope into the chairman's palm.

"For your fuel sir", he whispered.

The financial contribution promised by the secretary was not forth-coming while inaccessibility deepened. Everyday, Mr. Ejeme was at the state capital trying to discover possible avenues for lobbying. Since the probe order was given by the governor, it was most unlikely that the panel would turn in inaccurate findings, but if the chairman was handsomely gratified, the findings could be couched in such a way that the penalty would not assume unbearable magnitude. The biggest huddle however remained the panel secretary who wouldn't condone such vicious gratification. So Vero lost hope of getting relief from Mr. Ejeme.

Ten days after the awful revelation, Willie was still unable to decide on that to do. His thinking faculty was stretched to capacity. By the sixteenth day he had dismissed rationality and opted for expediency. He was convinced beyond doubt that he was not the father of the expected baby, and so repudiated the idea of starting married life with a weak compromise that was prone to weak snapping with the slightest disaffection.

Vero had a premonition of inhospitable treatment from Willie but found no basis for that fear. She arrived at Willie's station before mid-day on the dooms day. As soon as she entered his room, he woke up from day-dreaming and brightened up suddenly. Vero noticed the quick switch from a glum mood to a vivacious one.

"Willie, I hope you are quite well."

"Certainly, I got up from siesta a few minutes ago. When I have a long nap, I look stupid on getting up, hence I engage in it only when I must!

"I thought you were thinking of your problems, engagements and plans for the future".

"Thanks to goodness I have very few problems."

"Aren't you blessed you have very few problems?"

"You are either being ironical or mocking my naïve claim. A man is naturally supposed to hare more problems than a woman."

"It depends on individual circumstances. I personally have more problems than an average man."

"You who have number two man in your local government area as your friend and every woman's darling as your fiancé."

The pain of reminding her of better-forgotten affair with the secretary overshadowed the joy the latter part of the statement should evoke, thereby re-awakening her fear that Willie did not credit her with credibility when she declared that her friendship with the secretary was a past event which should be ascribed to youthful exuberance. She frowned deeply and instantly became melancholic. Willie didn't give her the chance to voice her objection.

"You have become so touchy of late. Every remark hurts you."

"What a naughty man you are. You don't care a fig about people's feelings. You provoked carelessly and wouldn't allow the provoked to register her protest. Yes, I have grown irritable; who touched off the irritability?"

"I do not believe my remark is offensive enough to evoke this angry reaction. If there is any grudge bothering your mind, please unburden yourself. I never intended to hurt your feelings."

"Please don't mention the secretary to me anymore. Women's waywardness is indelible; men have a licence to indulge in amorous adventures," said Vero sarcastically.

Willie laughed vibrantly. "Are you becoming jealous of men?"

"I am not. I know this is the world of men but do not forget that women are mortal like men and that it is only divine spirits that are free from weaknesses. Women have been relegated enough."

"I have taken note of your plea for women generally". With this, geniality re-surfaced in their companionship.

"Thanks for your hospitality Willie. I must leave. You men are callus. You do not have the goodness to ask how I am nurturing the seed you planted in me. It takes two to be pregnant but the burden is borne by one; another masculine privilege which I do not begrudge, but verbal expression of sympathy alone will soothe the strain."

"I am sorry darling. I do not see any adverse effect on your appearance. I should be obliged if you would spare another five minutes".

Vero sat back but not in a relaxed posture. That day she had recurrent fear which she could not account for.

"What I am going to say has depressed me for so long that unless I open up candidly, I will not enjoy peace of mind. Rather than deliberately offend you, I am trying to remove a possible source of disaffection between us when we settle down as a married couple. I have subjected myself to severe self-examination, carefully analyzed the circumstances surrounding our association and come to the conclusion that I am not responsible for your pregnancy. By this I do not mean that we shall forthwith call off our engagement unless you think otherwise. If we could look into the egg and identify its sex, our headache would be over soon. I do not want to own a son of doubtful identity, a first son for that matter ..."

She didn't allow him to continue. The foreboding had actualized itself. "Thank you for your genial frankness. Good night."

She moved out in a flash without looking at Willie. As soon as she entered her room, she bolted her door and started crying. The dissipation tired her out so much that she sat on the floor, resting her head on the rail of her bed throughout the night. When she stopped crying, she objectively re-assessed her relationship with Mr. Ejeme, her parents and Willie. Her mother's statement you will want a husband when you cannot get one – jarred her in the face. Would she go at once to her parents and plead for forgiveness? That wouldn't solve the problem. The fact that she had a pregnancy outside wedlock would enkindle their abhorrence. Even if they forgave her in spite of everything, did this stamp of defeat not render her unmarriageable by men who had a taste?"

What had her blind association with a married man brought her other than regrets and perennial problem? The secretary now had enough of his own problems. Even if he had none, would he claim this unlawful child? Most painful of all, who would help her bring up the child when born? Now that Willie had boldly disowned the unborn baby, what chances of winning him back were left to her? It appeared to her an all-round hopeless case.

Why not swallow her pride if she had any left, go back to Willie, prostrate herself before him and offer to accept any condition provided he provided her a shield from public ridicule and the eventual curse of her parents? If she owned up now, wouldn't that portray her as a liar who should be written off as unreliable? Willie jilted girls without a stain what more a person with a publicised blemish? Willie said he wouldn't accept an illegitimate child. What if they patched up their relationship and eventually she gave birth to a baby-boy?

Abortion was out of the question since no doctor worth his name would risk aborting a five-month old pregnancy. What would provide her a cover from public glare? She cursed the day she knew Mr. Ejeme and the authorities who made the relief program so unpalatable as to expose her to irresistible temptation. She thought of going to bare her mind to her pastor and perhaps find solace in renewing a clean relationship with her maker, but so long as the child lived, she would be continually reminded of her profligate life. Then came an over-riding question; where would he or she live – not in Michael's house-holds!

A few weeks later, the findings of the panel which probed Ikpem Local Government financial misappropriation were publicised. Among other punitive measures against the offending officials, the education secretary was demoted and was to refund a huge sum of money in monthly installments to be deducted from his salary at source. Before he and his wife absorbed the shock, the news of Vero's pregnancy gained currency throughout the local government area. There was no gain-saying. The verdict of guilt against the secretary was unanimous. This verdict cost him the little sympathy his wife had for him. At school she was most miserable. The Vero - Secretary episode was a household discussion for weeks. Her fellow female teachers never spared her embarrassment.

Back at home she nagged bitterly and ceaselessly. Mr. Ejeme was denuded completely of the power of defence. Night and day sleep deserted his eyes. Food became a tasteless pill which must be forced down the throat to preserve life. Why preserve this life if he remained a living dead? His Christian conscience warned him:

"You are at variance with your God. Death for you now is death indeed. This present predicament of yours is not going to be a permanent feature of your life. Perhaps it has a vital lesson to teach you. If you heed the voice of reason, you will refrain from rash action and gradually rebuild your crumbling life and family."

Alone he nourished the resuscitating feeling; in the company of his wife, he became a convict of self-indictment. Sometimes the nagging became more relieving than exasperating for it offered him an opportunity to listen to the voice of a loved one whose sole aim was to reclaim a straying partner, thus retrieving him from relapses into eerie recollection of irrationality and guilt. Although the repeated reprimands invariably re-enacted his offences old and recent, venial and culpable, forgiven and forgotten, he perceived in them self-less love and lawful protest.

Vero's rejection by her father's household was total. Even her youngest brother whom she lovingly cared for when she still had her family's love never thought of giving her the honour of a casual visit. She accepted the rejection and effaced the memory of the relations from her mind. With her apparent abandonment by dependable friends, especially Hilda whose comradeship and sympathy were badly desired now, she felt an irresistible urge to mend fences with her family, but she lacked the will-power to take a plunge. She had avoided them so long that she needed a go-between to renegotiate a fresh rapport.

Fate and procrastination robbed her of the chance of achieving the reconciliation. Not quite one week after the dramatic parting of ways with Willie, Sylvester, Vero's youngest brother, appeared from the blue. Seeing him from the door way, she hurried out to welcome him. Perhaps her parents had changed their mind about her. She took him by the hand and asked:

"Sylva, what brought you here today?" …smiling more than she was disposed to within that period. Before he had time to answer the question, she had asked another one.

"How are Papa and Mama? I hope there is no problem at home".

"Yes, Papa had a stroke yesterday", he replied artlessly. Frightened out of her wits she added: "Is the attack serious? Where is he hospitalized?"

"He was taken to the maternity home near our village for first aid treatment. He was there before I left but the nursing sister in charge advised that he should be sent to the general hospital. Mother ordered me to come and inform you."

She was surprised that the little boy did not give way to emotion; she managed to contain her own emotional weakness. She thought fast. Much as she desired to go home at once, and it was most sensible, she felt, and rightly too, that the shock of beholding her protruding abdomen would cause the tenuous link between her father and life to snap. She reached for a hand bag hanging on the wall, pulled out a full-scarp envelope and stuffed it with some money.

"Give this to Mama and tell her I will be home before mid-day. Let them send him to the general hospital at once."

As soon as the boy was out of her sight, she closed her door and started crying once more. Her mind, distilled by tension was unable to fashion out any line of action. She quickly concluded that her moral laxity, improvident life style and absolute lack of concern for the family's financial needs must have been contributory factors to her fathers' hypertension. If she went home in her present state, she would complicate matters. On the other hand, not going home would be interpreted as satanic nonchalance by her mother and other relations. She dried her tears and made an attempt at sorting out things soberly. Had she committed a crime that nobody else had committed before? She reflected on the circumstances of her up-bringing and the yet unresolved financial trauma of her education. Could there be a brand of ingratitude more horrible than that? She made a supplication to death to terminate "this state of hellish uneasiness", but found herself drained of the courage to endure the horror of gradual passing away. She thought of a less painful death. She picked up a piece of paper and scribbled a suicide note:

"I am to blame for whatever went wrong in my personal affairs and my family. I realized the stark truth too late. I have a strong feeling that Papa will not survive this bout of stroke and I cannot stand my mother's cold stare. I crave God's forgiveness but I treasure my father's. If only my death would restore Papa to life. If Hilda will ever forgive me, let her take care of Mama."

Folding the piece of paper and addressing it to 'Mama,' she placed it on her table beside the remnants of the dozen tablets of a sedative she took.